DAVE LAWSON

THE PAWNS OF HAVOC

AN ENVOYS OF CHAOS NOVELLA

For Audrie, who's always believed in my characters.
I'm sorry that Tobias isn't in this one.

THE SEA OF DREAD
ELLI
TU
GECHELD
TRUNEL
CURNELL
KILNIC

CAYL
ILA
THE FROZEN LANDS
KOSEL
TORR'S RIVER

PART ONE:

THE TEAM ASSEMBLES

First, the coughing started, then the blood. Cork heated water and prepared rags, knowing it would only get worse. It was this way every night. His mother would eat dinner, laughing as she drank her daily glass of Trunellic whiskey, her eyes flashing with vitality. Alive. Tonight, she'd even mustered the strength to use her mage powers and boil up some water for tea. She rarely had the energy these days to use her abilities.

Within an hour of eating, she was hunched on the floor, her body convulsing as the coughing overtook her. Blood seeped from her nostrils, running down her mouth and dripping onto her frock. In the rare moments she opened her eyes, they were glassy and dead. New sores emerged from the scars that covered her arms and neck—angry red boils, reeking of death.

Cork couldn't look at her. Not for more than a few moments. The woman who'd been so strong in his childhood, now so weak she struggled to walk across a room. He picked her up and carried her to her bed, placing her gently on the lumpy mattress and covering her legs and waist with a threadbare wool blanket.

The room was stark. A bed, an oil lamp, and a jug of water. On the wall, a painting of Cork his mother had done a few years previously. He'd posed for hours, dressed for battle, resting his greataxe on his shoulder. When she had the strength, his mother's skill with a brush was undeniable.

She needed a medic. They couldn't cure her but could lessen the symptoms. There was a remedy, but that involved traveling back to the Isle, something Cork's mother refused to do.

"They didn't give me a Kirth's bit of help when I left," she'd say every time he asked. "Why would I trust them now?" On her good days, she'd place an arm on his shoulder and give him a reassuring squeeze. "Besides, I've got you here, don't I? And yer da. Don't need no bloody Winn interfering with our lives."

Cork grimaced at the mention of the Winn, his mother's people. The most powerful mages he knew and a bunch of creepy buggers.

"Wouldn't hurt to ask 'em, Mum."

"No, lad—" A hacking cough sent his mother into a fit. She lay on the floor, writhing, blood leaking from her mouth. Cork stared, impotent with rage. Angry at the Winn for doing this to his mother, angry at his father for sitting by and doing nothing, angry at himself for being so godsdamned useless. And, even though he hated himself for it, angry at his mother for being sick.

After a few minutes, his mother inhaled slowly and sat up, wiping the still-flowing blood from her lips. "Leave the Winn out of this."

Once his mother made up her mind, there was no changing it. Cork's father had long since come to that realization and silently went about his work as a tanner. The man rarely spoke these days. He either worked, drank, or slept.

This evening, the bleeding was worse than usual, and within minutes, the front of Cork's mother's dress was soaked through with dark red.

"I'm goin' ta find a way, Mum," Cork promised. He took his mother's hand and squeezed. "Just need ya to hold on a bit longer. The medic will be here soon."

She nodded and gave his hand a light squeeze. All the strength she had left. Soon, she was asleep, snoring softly amidst fits of wheezing.

Cork stayed at her side until the medic, a thin weed of a man, arrived and began administering his treatments. First an ointment for Cork's mother's throat to soothe the cough, then a tonic to ease the pain and slow the bleeding. His mother woke up long enough to choke the tonic down and then fell back asleep while the medic finished.

Finally, the medic stood and sighed. "There's nothing I can do for the sores except keep them clean. She'll have less pain for a few days." The medic's eyes flitted to Cork's arms, scanning the Dreamshapes that covered them. "I wish I could do more. The only cure—"

"I know," Cork said. *Gods, do I know.* "Thank ya." Cork handed the man a small purse of silver crowns. After a quick bow, the medic left.

Cork sat by his mother, monitoring her breathing, wishing she would listen to him and go back to the Isle. Life there couldn't be worse than this long, slow death.

Lost in his thoughts, Cork sat by his mother's side until the first light of the two morning suns. He yawned, but sleep would have to wait. Sleep didn't pay the medic's weekly bill.

No, he'd have to make the best of it. Nothing to do but go to work. And work, that's what Cork did best.

Cork brushed sweat from his brow as he walked through the streets of Kilnic, heading for the Cross, Meldred's headquarters. Cork had worked for Meldred for a few years now, ever since turning fifteen, and he'd never seen the man anywhere but the Cross.

Kilnic had grown since Cork had moved there as a child. The streets that were once filled with cattle now bustled with merchants and well-dressed women browsing the wares of dress shops. The air smelled of perfumes and wildflowers, which had to be imported from the south. Nothing that beautiful grew this far north.

Stepping out of the way of a carriage, Cork bumped into a fine-looking woman in a maid's frock.

"Oi!" The maid's coarse voice had an appealing huskiness about it. Anger flashed across her face before she focused on the thin scar that traveled the length of the left side of Cork's cleanly shaven face. Her expression softened, and her eyes moved down to his torso. "Well, hello there."

"Well, 'ello." Cork took the woman's hand in his and went down for a kiss. "I'm Cork."

The maid stiffened and let out a strangled gasp. She stared at Cork's arms. Muscular, tanned, and covered in Dreamshapes. Swirling black tattoos that marked him as Winn.

"I must go." The maid pulled her hand away and rushed away, not looking back.

Kirth's bollocks. Cork hadn't been back to the Isle since his parents had immigrated to Trunel, and yet he'd never escape this. The so-called decent people of Sarakan treating him like a monster. Like he was off building armies of enhanced wolves bred to devour entire nations, eating babies, or stealing away women for breeding stock. Cork had heard all the rumors, and they were lies. Mostly.

Cork moved past a merchant and an imperiously dressed noblewoman—all white hair and floral print, a permanent scowl on her face—who argued about the price of a fuchsia gown. Old Town Kilnic didn't have enough weaponsmiths. Too many dresses, not enough steel. No one ever killed anyone with a dress.

While he walked, Cork noticed the stares. A young mother's terrified eyes on him as she shepherded her children across the street and into a shop, whispering, "Shh, those nasty Winn eat naughty children." A man in a fine frock coat pretended to be fascinated by a tavern sign, but every few moments, he shot a look toward Cork.

The imperious woman paused in her argument long enough to look down at Cork through her eyeglasses, fixing a scandalized glare on him. "Oh gods, a Winn? Here in Kilnic? How beastly. I must return to Dramin at once."

Cork nodded to her. "Get buggered," he said in his kindest voice.

The women huffed loudly and scurried away.

The merchant focused his anger on Cork now. "You just cost me three hundred damn crowns, you Winn bastard. I hope one of yer bloody warwolves bites your manhood off."

With a shrug, Cork continued on his way.

Being feared wasn't terrible, most of the time. Cork didn't have to deal with as many toffs and dandies and their tedious small talk and backhanded compliments. However, no matter how much he rationalized the benefits, being the object of fear and disgust made him wonder about himself. He tried to be kind and only killed when someone paid him to, and yet the people of Kilnic would never accept him as a person.

Perhaps he was a monster, after all? Perhaps the toffs and well-dressed women were correct. He wasn't worth knowing.

Cork pushed those thoughts aside as he arrived at the Cross, aptly named, as the tavern sat at the crossroads of the two main boulevards of Kilnic. A small wooden shack of a building on the outside, but once you walked through the tattered doors, the tavern had a homey feel. It wasn't fancy, but it was clean. A mustachioed bartender stood behind the polished solid oak bar that was stained chocolate brown like the three tables in the center of the Cross. The air smelled of sausages and ale. Cork smiled, his mouth watering. It had been a while since his last meal.

Meldred sat at the furthest of the three tables, sipping at an overflowing mug of foamy ale. Next to him sat a woman dressed in men's trousers and a black leather tunic. She was sickly thin; she'd barely reach Cork's ribs if she stood next to him. Short, spiky hair made her head look like a mace, and she glowered at Cork as if she hated him. And not because of the Dreamshapes. She looked him straight in the eye with no sign of fear or disgust. Just anger.

Cork raised his hand in greeting. "I'm Cork."

"Kirth take you, Cork," the woman said.

Cork eyed Meldred, as if to ask why this pleasant young woman was there. And why was she so damned angry?

"Now, Nessa," Meldred said in good humor. "Let the man sit."

Nessa scowled but said nothing.

Cork nodded to Meldred and sat at the table. "Yer note said there was a job?"

Meldred's eyes lit up. He took a large swig of ale and began. "Yes, my boy, a job sent straight from the heavens. The Swordsman looks down on us with favor today."

Cork tried not to react. He'd known Meldred long enough to realize that the man always talked up a mission beforehand, even with the most tedious jobs. Meldred was a decent man for a mercenary. He treated his employees well, avoided the obviously criminal jobs, and most importantly, always paid what he owed. However, he was still a business-man. He'd tell his employees all the positives first and only discuss the negative aspects if needed.

"What's the job?" Cork asked.

Meldred hesitated, taking a sip of ale. "We can't afford to reject this one, Cork. It'll feed us for years. May not make us rich, but it will make us comfortable."

Nessa stared at Cork, as if planning what her first move would be. A dagger to the heart or to the throat? She looked like a dagger-wielder. With her slight frame, she couldn't overpower a child, but she'd be agile, sneak through defenses, and plunge her weapon home.

"The job?" Cork kept his eyes trained on Meldred.

"You won't like it," Meldred said. He took another sip of his ale, then clasped his hands together. "We've been hired to destroy a convoy."

"Easy enough," Cork said. His shoulders relaxed. He hadn't even realized how tense they were. A convoy was an afternoon's work, at most. Not worth the kind of money Meldred had mentioned. "What's the catch?"

"You can't steal anything. Just destroy all the supplies."

"Turnos' tits," Nessa hissed. "I'll steal if I wish." She reached into a pocket and brought forth a dagger, stabbing the table with it.

"Daggers, bleedin' knew it." It took Cork a moment to realize he'd spoken aloud.

"What?" Nessa's eyes bore into him.

Cork, get yer head outta yer ass. "Yer daggers...they're...uh...nice, like."

"Get buggered." Nessa pushed the dagger further into the wood.

Meldred glared at Nessa. "I love your enthusiasm, my dear, but these tables were godsdamn expensive, and I have no desire to replace them." He motioned toward the back door of the Cross. "If you wish to practice with your little knives, be a dear and go out into the alley."

Nessa stood abruptly, knocking her chair over. She stormed out, muttering questions about what kind of arseholes wouldn't allow stealing.

"Lovely girl," Cork said, watching the door. Hopefully Nessa would get lost out there and wouldn't return. "Wouldn't want to meet her in a dark alley."

"Indeed. However, despite her undeniable charms, she's necessary."

"How?" Cork crossed his arms. "A group of the men and I can take out a bloody convoy. Ain't no big worry, that."

"You won't have any of the men," Meldred said. "Our employer requires that this be done in secret. You'll travel by carriage. You, Nessa, and one other, an archer. You'll destroy the convoy and supplies." Meldred hesitated, looking Cork in the eye. "And then you will kill every member of the convoy except one. Our employers require one survivor to spread word of the attack."

"I ain't no executioner." Cork folded his arms across his wide chest.

"No, but our friend Nessa is."

"I'm confused. Why do they want a survivor? What's the convoy carrying?"

Meldred shrugged. "I don't know, but for what they're paying us, I'll gladly be confused. They asked for you specifically, though."

"Who are these bastards?"

"Your old friends," Meldred said, looking at Cork's forearms. "Emissaries of the Isle of Winn."

Cork couldn't speak for several moments. The Winn. Mages who could kill you with the flick of a wrist, calling up barrages of ice. His people. Well, former people. The reason his mother could barely walk most evenings. And they wanted to hire him?

"Kirth's bloody shittin' bollocks," Cork said. He placed his hands on the table to steady himself.

"Eloquently put." Meldred smirked. "However, for the money they're paying, I wouldn't care if they were cannibals from the depths of the Dark Beyond. I'd just smile and nod and get the money."

The money would be nice, Cork admitted. He'd be able to pay for a medic, get his mother into a house out in the country. Out of the teeming arsehole of Kilnic's lower quarter.

"I'm telling you this, Cork, because they specifically asked for you. But they made it clear they don't want anyone beyond you and me to know. That means Nessa."

"Understood." Cork gave a small laugh. Nessa wouldn't care anyway, based on Cork's initial impression. "What about our third?"

Meldred grimaced. "Ah, you'll want to get Nessa first before we talk about that. There's been a complication."

When Cork reached the alleyway, Nessa sat amongst the filth of an absent beggar's tattered blanket, throwing daggers at the wall.

"Is the wall dead yet?" Cork asked.

Nessa regarded him with disdain and held a dagger out, as if she wished to throw it at him. "What?" Nessa gripped the dagger tighter.

"Boss wants you to come back in. Says we's got a problem."

"I thought there'd be less talking and more killing." Nessa got to her feet and brushed the dirt off her trousers.

Cork ignored her, turning and reentering the Cross.

"Well?" Meldred eyed the door.

"Comin'," Cork grunted. By the time Cork sat and sipped at his quickly warming ale, Nessa had slunk through the door, noiselessly gliding across the Cross and into her seat. *A silent killer, that one.*

Nessa glowered at Meldred. "What's the problem?"

"Ah, the third member of your crew has met with a bit of difficulty." Meldred gave them a worried smile. "In order for her to join you on this job, you'll need to help extricate her from this bit of trouble."

Nessa scowled. "Do I know her? Care about her? No. I don't give a shit if she dies."

"Nessa—" Meldred began.

"Unless she's personally paying my wages, she can go straight to Kirth."

"Who is she?" Cork asked. He'd had enough of Nessa and her incessant complaints.

"You won't like that answer, either," Meldred said.

Turnos' tits. "You hired *her*?"

Meldred winced. "She's a good shot."

"She's got no idea what she's bleedin' doin'."

"Who in Kirth is 'her?'" Nessa asked.

"Arabella." Cork sighed, thinking of the one time he'd worked alongside her. The company had made camp for the night, and she'd been shooting arrows into the trees as a bit of a laugh. Cork had stepped into the trees for a piss and had almost ended up with an arrow in his back. "She's a pain in the arse."

Cork and Nessa followed Meldred's directions to the north end of Old Town, near the warehouse district. Cork had expected Arabella to live in a small house or a rented room. Instead, they arrived at a storefront adorned with a wooden sign proclaiming Howston and Son's Cobbler Shop. The shop itself looked well-kept, with wooden siding atop a stone frame, green shutters decorating the two upstairs windows, and a portico covering the entrance from the elements.

The issue at hand was immediately clear. Three men stood under the portico, gesturing angrily to each other. The tallest of the three had a long black beard and the hard, weathered facial features of a sailor or dockhand, his skin wrinkled leather. The shortest of the three was godsdamned ugly. Scrunched features, a bulbous nose, sunken eyes, and a few scraggly blonde hairs hanging limp from his chin. No more than a year older than Cork but already balding. The third man was average in every sense of the word except for an enormous belly protruding from his relatively small chest and arms. He stood almost completely still while the other men muttered and banged on the door furiously.

Cork was at least a head taller than all of them and bigger. Three against one might be difficult, but perhaps Nessa would stop sulking and show her own skills.

"A nice day, ain't it?" Cork asked. He nodded and gave the men a genial smile.

"Wot do you want?" The bearded man sneered menacingly at Cork.

"Just a conversation. About weather and the like."

"Go cut yer bollocks off," the short man said. He had a screeching voice that immediately annoyed Cork.

"Sounds painful." Cork gestured to the house. "Don't seem like the residents want to see ya."

"Oh, they'll see us, all right."

"Menacing remarks. Man after my own heart. Yer a sailor, ain't ya?"

"What's it to you?" The man's eyes widened, showing Cork had guessed right.

"I'm gonna call you Sailor, then." Cork nodded to the shortest man. "Yer little friend can be Shorty." A wink at the big-bellied man. "He's Belly, of course." He gave the men his biggest grin. "I'm here to help you boys."

"How's you gonna do that?" Shorty's hand moved closer to his sword.

Cork patted his back harness where his greataxe lay sheathed. "I'm pretty good with an axe." He pointed to Nessa sitting under a nearby tree, carving something into the bark. "And my friend over there. Wonderful artist. Carves trees." Cork spat on the ground. "And people."

"We don't need yer help," Sailor said. "There's one bloody woman in there. Easy work."

"And yet yer standing out here, still, staring at the door."

Shorty glared at him. "I ain't that short!"

Cork snorted.

"She's got a bow," Shorty continued.

"Aye, that is a problem." Cork smiled. Yes, Arabella indeed had a bow. She was an excellent shot, and gods, she knew it. Cork had only worked with her once before, but she'd spent the entire job showing off her markswoman skills to the entire company. Cork had wanted nothing to do with her. Showing off did nothing for you in battle. It usually killed you and those around you. And now, not only did Cork have to work with her, he also had to save her.

Swordman's bloody bollocks.

Cork stepped back from the men to where he could see the upstairs window. Shorty looked like he wanted to say something, but Sailor gave him a warning glance. Still leaning against the wall, Belly seemed asleep.

"Let me try something," Cork said. "Arabella?" he called. The curtain twitched open a hair, and an arrow whizzed through the air, hitting the ground a few paces from Cork's feet. "Good to see you, too, lass. These men down here seem to want to see ya."

No response. The curtain closed.

"That's right," Sailor said. "She owes us three hundred crowns."

"Why don't ya just pay the nice men?"

Arabella's crisp voice sounded from above. "The nice men deserve an arrow through the throat."

"Thanks for yer help." Cork stepped back under the portico.

"See." Sailor gestured upward. "She's a godsdamned menace. As soon as we showed up, she started shooting at us. We hadn't even threatened her yet."

"Rude of her." Cork gave the men his most innocent grin. "Look, we can work this out. You know Meldred?"

The men exchanged glances, furrowing their brows. "Course we do," Sailor said. "Everyone does."

Cork's grin widened. "He'll pay ya the money Arabella owes you. May even have a job for ya."

"Don't want no jobs." Shorty crossed his arms. "We's got 'em already."

Sailor nodded his agreement. "Ain't about the money. S'bout the principle. You get a loan, you don't pay it back, you lose your godsdamned arms. Everyone knows that."

"Normally I'd agree with ya," Cork said, "but I's need Arabella here. Fer a job. Meldred's job. He'd be bleedin' pissed if we's keep having delays. I'd happily cut her guts out with ya on another day, but now? We's don't got time for this."

Belly grunted. Apparently, he was not a statue after all. "We'll say how much time we've got," he said in a gravelly voice.

"That won't work," Cork said. The men reached for their swords. "Nessa, ya might want to help." Cork reached for his axe.

Nessa remained seated under the tree. "Not my issue."

Three against one. Cork had done it before, but the odds weren't good. However, the men were more thugs than soldiers. Muscular, well-armed, but without the discipline needed on the battlefield. They clumped up against the front of the cobbler shop, hesitant to leave the safety of the portico.

Cork could either step back and force them to enter the path of Arabella's arrows or use the close quarters to his advantage.

He chose both.

With a quick motion, he grabbed the greataxe from behind his right shoulder and kicked out, his boot connecting with Belly's stomach. The man slumped against the door and landed on his backside with a grunt. Before he could get up or the other men could unsheathe their weapons, Cork stepped back off the porch into the yard.

Let the men come to him. And if one of them got an arrow from Arabella for his troubles, that'd make things easier.

"Nessa," Cork ordered through gritted teeth. "I want ya to bleedin' help."

"No," Nessa said, still sitting under the tree, watching the scene dispassionately.

"Got yerself quite the companion, don't ya?" Shorty asked as he moved forward, a shortsword in each hand.

Cork sighed. "Two of 'em." He looked up at Arabella's window. "Not sure which is worse."

Cork swung the axe in a heavy cut against the Shorty's swords. The man parried the blow, but Cork brought the pommel into his face, crushing the man's nose. As Shorty dropped a sword and reached up to his face, Cork grabbed him by the shoulder and flung him into the yard. The swish of an arrow and a dull thunk told Cork that Arabella had found her mark.

The other two men looked at Cork with more concern now, a touch of panic in their eyes. Had Shorty been their best fighter? If so, this fight wouldn't last much longer.

"You can surrender if ya like," Cork said. "Don't got to die today."

"I'll cut yer bollocks off," Sailor said, shaking his long sword in what was supposed to be a menacing fashion. Instead, it just made Cork laugh, watching the sword go up and down.

"Have it yer way." Cork stepped forward, lifting his axe above his right shoulder. With a grunt, he heaved the axe forward, bringing it down toward Belly's head. The man blocked the cut but had to step back.

Keep them off balance. Don't let them get into a rhythm. Each cut or thrust didn't matter. Cork didn't need a quick win. He'd been swinging his axe for years now, and he'd built up endurance.

Let the men stay back, waiting for Cork to slip or lose focus or get tired. It wouldn't happen. It might have worked a few years before, but now, Cork was disciplined. No one would have considered him thoughtful—he was a big, hulking bastard with an axe after all, not the kind of person people assumed was a philosopher—but in battle, Cork analyzed every aspect. Watching for openings in his opponents' defenses, preying on their anxiety and worry. A scared enemy was an easier kill.

"Kroomashus," Cork said. One of the several Winn words his mother had taught him. It meant the birth of a boy child, but the men didn't know that. As far as they were concerned, he was a child-murdering cannibal. "Kroomashus, krooma." Cork gave the men a wicked smile.

"What are you saying?" Sailor asked, eyes wide in terror.

"He's bloody cursing us." Belly tried to step further back, but he was already against the shop exterior. "He's a Winn mage!"

"Kroomashus." Cork held the axe in one hand, freeing the other to continue the charade. He lifted the free hand and began to twirl it, like he'd seen mages do. "Kroomashus vida."

"Kill 'im!" The two men charged.

Cork took his axe in both hands again and cut across the men, knocking them into each other. He took the pommel and jammed it into Belly's face. As the man fell, Cork kicked out at Sailor, keeping him at bay long enough to take a step back and bring his axe down through Belly's skull. Blood sprayed, and the blade squelched as it split halfway through the man's head.

Sailor sat on his knees, consumed by fear, gaping at Cork, who loomed above him. The man had dropped his sword. He waited for his own execution.

"Get up," Cork said.

"Just do it," the man said. "Kill me."

As Cork lifted his axe, something twinged in his gut. He gripped the hilt tighter, thinking of his earlier conversation with Meldred. Of all the killing he'd soon have to do. "No," Cork said. "Ya get to live."

Sailor's eyes filled with confusion. "What? Why?"

"Go to yer employer and let 'em know that Arabella's debt is paid." Cork placed the flat of the axehead against the man's forehead. "No one will ever come back to bother her or anyone in Meldred's service." Cork removed his axe and grinned down at the man. "And if I's see you again, or any harm comes to any of my people, I'll slice your worthless corpse into pieces."

The man nodded. "Thank you, sir."

Cork gestured toward the yard. "Now leave."

Sailor's eyes flicked up toward the window. "What about the woman? With the bow."

"Arabella," Cork called.

"Yes?" came the response.

"We're letting him go."

"What? But he wants to kill me."

"Not anymore. He's actually hoping ya live forever."

"Okay," Arabella said, though she sounded unconvinced.

Cork nodded toward the yard. "Well?" he asked Sailor.

The man stood and fled.

Nessa, from underneath her tree, watched him leave and then eyed Cork. "Should have killed him."

"Figured I'd let him take the message back to his employer."

"Naïve." Nessa turned back to the tree and continued carving.

I ain't no executioner.

Muffled footsteps from inside the house brought Cork out of his thoughts. He kicked Belly's corpse out of the doorway and stepped to the side as Arabella sauntered out of the house.

She wore a light blue chiffon dress with a fur cloak draped over it, looking more like a debutante at a nobleman's ball than a mercenary archer descending from a cobbler's shop. Her auburn hair curled into ringlets around her shoulders and shined in the light of the two suns.

Arabella gave Cork a slight curtsy, an assured smile on her tanned face. The tan was the only part of her appearance that gave away her working-class roots. "Thank you," Arabella said in a calm voice. "All that wasn't necessary, though. I had the situation under control."

Nessa scoffed. She'd moved to the bodies and rifled through their pockets. "If your goal was dying."

Arabella regarded Nessa with a cool glare, the image of an aristocratic young lady. "Hardly."

Cork looked Arabella up and down and pointed to the shop's sign, two golden boots painted onto a wooden board. "Didn't reckon you for a cobbler."

"I'm not." Arabella's brow furrowed. Her lips curled in disgust.

"Just spending yer time at cobbler's shops then?" Cork's lips curled into a sly grin. "Marrying yerself a cobbler?"

"My boots need fixing," Nessa said. She lifted one leg, displaying the mess of frayed leather and string she called boots.

"Go find my father, then," Arabella bit out. "This is his shop."

"How does a cobbler's daughter learn to use a bow?" Cork asked.

"Practice." Arabella swept past him and walked toward the road. The gravel crunched beneath the unmarred soles of her expertly crafted boots as she turned back to Cork and gave an expectant look. "If you're done asking questions, perhaps we could make our way back to Meldred?"

Cork scowled. He'd saved her godsdamned life, and she was acting like she'd deserved nothing less. "Fine." He looked to Nessa, who still knelt in front of the corpses. "Coming?"

"I'll meet you there," Nessa said, searching through the Belly's trouser pockets. "Still got another body to search."

Within moments, Cork found himself cursing Arabella's name even more. She walked at a brisk pace, forcing Cork to match her speed. His stride was much longer, but he was at least twice her weight and didn't walk much faster than an amble most days. A carriage clattered along on the cobblestones of the surprisingly empty street. Early evening in Kilnic was usually full of cheering drunks parading the thoroughfare searching for further diversions, either women or more liquor.

Cork stumbled on a jagged cobblestone and had to pause to steady himself. Arabella walked on as if he hadn't stopped. It would be too much to ask for her to walk at a decent pace like a normal person. Thankfully, they walked most of the way back to the Cross in silence—the only positive of rushing down the street. When they were within a few hundred paces, Arabella stopped in the middle of the road in front of a blacksmith shop. She turned to Cork and grimaced, as if she dreaded what she was about to do.

"Look, Connick. Your name is Connick, right?" Arabella asked.

"Cork."

Arabella frowned. "Pity. I like Connick better." She crossed her arms. "I do want to thank you. I would have dealt with those three louts eventually, but you certainly helped speed the situation up. And lessened the chances of me meeting an untimely end."

"Part of the job." Cork admired Arabella's beauty for a moment before pushing such thoughts from his head. She was pretty, yes, but frustrating, self-centered, and shallow. He did not want her to start showing kindness. Better to keep her at a distance and just steal a look at her now and then. Nothing good could come from getting to know her.

"Can we get out of the road? Even if ya feel like talkin', I'd rather not get run down by a bleedin' carriage."

He took her arm and led her to the edge of the road, next to the blacksmith's shop door. Iron hammers clanged again steel blades, the odor of burnt charcoal from the smithy oven filling the air.

Arabella regarded Cork's hand on her arm. Her skin was so damned delicate, Cork was hesitant to let go.

"Are we preparing to dance, Connick?"

"What?"

Arabella's lips curled into an amused smile. "You've taken my arm, so I assume we're dancing, but I don't hear the music. Unless you plan to frolic to the dulcet tones of hammers on iron."

Cork released Arabella's arm and averted his eyes. "Dunno what yer talkin' 'bout."

"Hmm. Perhaps another time, Master Connick." Her smile faded, and she bit her lip. "I wanted to ask, well, that is—"

"Spit it out." Cork spat on the ground, narrowly missing Arabella's white leather boots.

"I'm new to mercenary work." Arabella's eyes flickered to the blacksmith's shop.

"I'm not."

She gave a quick, nervous laugh. "I suppose I don't know what to expect."

"Pain." Cork kept his eyes on her, hoping she'd decide the mercenary life was not for her. "Death. And more sadness than I's can count."

"You certainly know how to talk to a girl," Arabella said, winking.

Sweet Torr's lips, she simply refused to let Cork's surly demeanor affect her. Cork grunted. Perhaps speaking made it seem like he cared what she had to say.

"Father wants me to be a cobbler," she continued as if Cork hadn't made a sound. "Marry a cobbler. Have cobbler children. All he thinks about are shoes. But I've wanted something more. To travel. See the world, perhaps visit Dramin." She trailed off, then bit her lip nervously. "That's why I became an archer. Mother taught me how to shoot, and my brother practiced with me."

"Ah." Cork hoped his curt tone would shut Arabella up so they could get on with the job.

"Meldred's been kind enough to give me a job. Doing me a favor, really. He and my mother were friends in their younger years. My mother is an excellent shot with a bow as well. She's better than me, but I'm better than my brother. I've only been on the one mission, and it was dreadfully boring. No action at all." Arabella looked up at Cork as if just now remembering he was there. "Have you been on many jobs?"

Cork peered down at her. "Yeah."

Arabella laughed. "Gods, you mercenaries are all so dreary. Your friend with the daggers looks like she wants to kill everyone in sight, and you can barely speak."

"I can speak," Cork said. "I's just know when not to."

"Ah well, your loss. People tell me I'm an excellent conversationalist."

"People are prone to lies."

"You have a touch of wit about you." Arabella turned to walk to the Cross. "You're full of surprises, Connick."

Cork cursed the gods.

When they reached the Cross, Arabella threw her arms around Meldred. "Uncle Melly," she cried.

Cork hid his face so Meldred wouldn't see his bemused expression. *Uncle Melly, huh?*

"Did Cork give you the rundown on the job, Ara?" Meldred asked, extricating himself from Arabella's embrace.

Arabella pouted. "No, he's barely said anything at all. And that woman with him said even less. What kind of people are you employing?"

"The kind that get shit done." Nessa entered the Cross carrying a satchel full of goods she'd looted from the men. "And shut up about it."

"She's right, Ara," Meldred said in a fatherly tone. "Cork and Nessa have proven their skills. You need to listen to them on this job. Do whatever they say. Don't be a bother."

She's already failed at that. "We're destroying a convoy," Cork said. "Out to the east."

"In the Frozen Lands," Meldred added.

Cork's eyes narrowed. That was new. "Ya hadn't mentioned the Frozen Lands before, Uncle Melly."

Meldred's eyes flashed in anger, but he regained composure. "Oh, didn't I? How silly of me." He leaned back and propped his legs up on the table and crossed his arms. "Yes, the Frozen Lands. Not very far into the Frozen Lands, mind you, but you may want to pack your warmest clothes."

"Yer wantin' us to camp in the Frozen Lands?" Cork gave Meldred an incredulous look. It made no sense. Spending more than a night in the Frozen Lands was the perfect way to die.

Meldred laughed mirthlessly. "No, boy. There are inns along the road. Maybe not in the Frozen Lands, but just outside."

Kirth. The Frozen Lands, as its name suggested, was a massive ice-covered tract of land to the northwest of Kilnic, along the Sea of Dread in northern Sarakan. Much of the Frozen Lands lay in Kosel, but the western edge was in Trunnelic territory. Cork had never been out that far to the northeast because, well, there wasn't much reason to. He'd been into Kosel on a few occasions, but the company had always avoided the extreme temperatures of the coastline, opting for the route along the Sarakan River to the south.

"So's we're taking the northern road?" Cork asked. "What kind of convoy travels the Frozen Lands this time of year?" The slightly less frigid Trunellic summer had passed a month before. and the harsher months of winter were on their way.

"Probably the kind that's trying to avoid being waylaid by marauders," Meldred said.

"Well, I'm sure I have a hundred better things to do before we leave." Arabella fiddled with the lacy sleeve of her dress. "I'll let the two of you discuss geography."

"Wait," Cork said. "We's need a strategy, like. Can't just go into the Frozen Lands and wait."

Nessa scowled. "You talk too much. We don't need a strategy. We're burning shit down. Killing some hapless bastards. I'll be back in a while. Maybe then you'll be ready to leave. In the meantime, maybe I'll take on a job."

"No," Meldred interjected. "Don't need you getting caught right before a job as big as this one."

Nessa gave Meldred an offended glare. "I don't get caught." She stormed out of the Cross, slamming the door behind her.

"I suppose I'll fetch my things as well," Arabella said. She made a hasty exit.

Meldred and Cork sat in silence for a few moments. Finally, Cork had had enough. "I's didn't know she could talk so much," he said.

"Arabella? Yes, indeed."

"No, Nessa. First time she's said more than three words."

"She talks a bit more when she's angry."

Cork crossed his arms. "She's always angry."

"Murderously angry."

"Point still stands." Cork stood. He'd need to gather his own supplies and be back at the Cross before Nessa and Arabella. If Nessa arrived first, gods knew what she'd do.

He wouldn't usually want a silent group when traveling on Meldred's business, but now he prayed to the Swordsman that it would be. Arabella was annoying, but a talking Nessa meant a greater likelihood of finding a dagger in his back.

"S'pose I'll get a meal before we leave," Cork said.

"Before you do that, there's someone waiting for you in the private rooms."

"Who?"

"Your countrymen."

Cork's heart thumped in his chest. "What are they bleedin' doin' here?"

Meldred gave a wan smile. "I didn't ask, my boy. They're quite grim, these Winn. Barely said three words and refused my offer of something for their dry throats. Odd buggers don't even drink."

Cork laughed. Winn certainly drank, but not when they were working. Cork decided he'd definitely need a large ale before heading out on this job and several more ales on the way. "Aye, they only drink blood, ya know."

Meldred narrowed his eyes. "You're lying. Right?" His lip trembled.

Cork winked. "Am I?"

He swept past Meldred toward the private rooms.

There were two Winn dressed in sweeping black robes, sitting serenely in two oak chairs near the fireplace. A man and a woman, both olive-skinned, with close-cropped black hair and Dreamshapes up and down their arms.

"You may call me Trellen Winn," the man said. "My companion is Yannel Winn. We come to speak to you."

"I figured," Cork said.

Yannel peered at Cork. "We know of your mother, Corkelle Winn." She motioned to an empty chair.

Cork remained standing, ignoring Yannel. "Aye, I reckon ya do." He gritted his teeth. There was so much he wanted to say to the bastards, but now wasn't the time.

"Her condition worsens," Yannel continued.

Cork nodded. Nothing to say there.

"If you complete this task for us, we'll accept her return to the Isle."

Cork couldn't help but laugh. "She ain't never goin' back there."

Trellen bared his teeth in what might have been a smile or a grimace. "Then we will supply you with the tonic to keep her symptoms at bay. She will live a normal life, though her mage abilities will fade."

"What?"

"The tonic is not the same as being one with the Flock, Corkelle Winn. She will lose her powers gradually, as is right for one who abandons the Flock."

Cork squeezed his fists together. It wouldn't do to punch the Winn in their sanctimonious throats. "That's not a shitein' normal life, is it?"

"It is as the Flock commands." Trellen cast his eyes downward. "Your mother shall live."

Cork inhaled deeply. He had to stay calm. "And alls I got to do is kill some people, eh?"

Yannel nodded. "We would prefer to never kill. Life is sacred. However, we must do what is best for our people. This convoy and its people, they are the sacrifice."

"Why leave one alive? Why not complete the sacrifice?"

Yannel eyed the ceiling, as if thinking. "We require a witness. Someone to bring news back to those who would defy our laws, showing them that we will not stand for their treachery."

Buncha miserable old bastards. "Yeah, makes total sense, that."

"You must not inform your companions of our involvement. It will not do for those not of the Flock to know of us."

I ain't part of yer damned Flock. Cork nodded. "Whatever ya say."

"You will stop at the inn in Ellid and wait. Our sources indicate an advance party of the convoy will arrive there to scout the way forward before returning to their brethren. Of course, such individuals must stay alive long enough to lead you back to the convoy, and then you will need to dispatch of them as well."

"Makes sense." Cork shrugged. What was a few more deaths, considering he'd be killing everyone else? "Any particular way you want 'em killed?" The Winn narrowed their eyes at him. "Sometimes the employers want us to get creative-like, ya know. Cut someone's bollocks out, stab out their eyes, make a necklace of their innards." Cork made a show of searching his pockets. "Got a dagger around here somewhere. You want I should cut their tongues out? Really send a message?"

Trellen stood, eyes blazing. "You disrespect the Flock."

Cork raised his hands in an appeasing manner. "No, no, just makin' a joke."

"We do not joke." Yannel's eyes bore into Cork's own.

Like I said, miserable bastards. Cork gave a shallow bow. "My apologies. Didn't want to disrespect the Flock. Flock's everything to me." The Winn sat, stone-faced. "Well, I guess I'll get started on the job, then. See ya around."

"The individuals you will kill are enemies of the Winn. They seek our destruction. You will not speak to your associates about this matter. Even your superiors." Yannel motioned to the door. "This Meldred fellow knows of our involvement, but not of our true purpose."

"Meldred ain't stupid."

"No, but he'll believe what he wants to believe. You shall inform him that we have told you of the financial gains the Winn seek and how we have asked you to destroy the convoy of a business rival. You will mention nothing else." Yannel smiled for the first time, an evil, toothy smirk. "Or your mother will never recover from her ailment, and we shall kill all your friends."

Cork's heart sunk into his stomach. "I don't like threats."

"These are not threats, only assurances of what would happen if you do not honor the Flock."

Cork closed his eyes and drew in a deep breath. "Fine. I'll do what you ask."

"Blessings," the two Winn intoned.

Meldred was waiting on the other side of the door, blinking rapidly, hands clenched. "Well, how'd it go?"

"Made some new friends, didn't I?" Cork stepped past Meldred toward the double doors of the Cross' exit.

"Wait, what did they say?"

"Nothin' much." Cork gave an exaggerated shrug. "Convoy's their business rivals. Winn don't like competition. They want us to stop in Ellid and wait there for the convoy's forward company."

"Why'd they need to speak to you privately?"

"They wanted me to rejoin 'em." Cork scoffed. "Might as well have saved themselves the trip." He motioned to the door. "I's better get the horses."

"No need. You'll be taking a carriage."

"What?"

"You're to take the public carriage. Dress like gentlefolk; avoid attention. Once you get out to the Frozen Lands, procure horses."

"What about weapons?"

"Pack those in your bags, put them on top of the carriage. I don't care either way."

Cork scowled. First the Winn, then having to work with Arabella and Nessa, now riding in a carriage, acting like a gentleman. "The Winn tell ya to have us ride in a carriage?"

Meldred's eyes twinkled with an evil gleam. "No, Cork, they've said nothing about that. I just like the idea of making you act like gentlefolk."

"Yer makin' this difficult for me, boss. Ya know that?"

Meldred nodded. "I know, but it will be worth it in the end." Cork turned to leave. "Oh, Cork. Do what you must. As long as the job gets done. Got the usual contacts in most of the towns along the way, so you shouldn't want for supplies or information if needed."

"Right, boss." And the Winn would also have people watching over them as well. So many monitoring their progress, but only the three of them doing the actual job. Seemed right wasteful. "I'll use the usual channels if I need to get in touch."

Meldred smiled. "Oh, and Cork. If your colleagues prove a hindrance, leave them behind in the Frozen Lands. It doesn't matter as long as we get our money."

"Leave your adopted niece to die?"

Meldred's smile turned into a toothy, leering grin. "You know what they say. Business before family."

PART TWO:

ANOTHER DAMNED COMPLICATION

ONCE THE SUPPLIES HAD been sorted and the carriage called, Cork met his unwanted companions outside the Cross. He'd meant to stop at his mother's rooms to say goodbye, but time had gotten away from him. So now, he'd just have to ask the coachman to stop along the way.

The carriage ambled down the thoroughfare, traversing the four blocks to Cork's mother's house, the buildings growing shabbier the further they traveled from the Cross.

"One moment, sir," Cork called to the carriage driver as they passed by his mother's residence. "I've got a quick errand to take care of."

"We's gotta be off for Ellid," the coachman protested.

"And we will be." Cork grinned. "It'll only take a moment." His grin turned serious. "And Meldred would be unhappy if I don't complete his orders here." He motioned to his mother's building.

The coachman swallowed nervously. "No need to bother Master Meldred. We'll be here waiting for your return, sir."

As Cork extricated himself from the carriage, Arabella favored him with a quizzical glance. "What's Uncle Melly got you doing now? Just as we're set to embark."

"I dunno." Cork shrugged. "He just said deliver some messages, and I said, 'Yessir.'"

Arabella opened her mouth to respond, but Cork shut the carriage door behind him, ending the conversation. *Bloody women.*

Cork's mother was sleeping when he entered her chambers. Faint snores accompanied by a pained wheezing, her nose dripping blood down her face and neck. Angry crimson sores had appeared on her arms, pushing against the skin and threatening to burst.

Cork shook her shoulder gently. "Mum." She coughed but still snored. "Mum." Her eyes opened. "I's got to go on a job."

His mother whimpered. "Cork," she whispered.

Cork took her hand in his. "Mum, this job will be the last one fer a while."

"Where?"

"Frozen Lands." Cork saw the fear in his mother's eyes. "Don't worry, it won't be dangerous." He gave her a reassuring smile. "And it's gonna save ya. The Winn, Mum. They hired me, and when the job's done, we'll have all the tonic we need. Ya won't be sick anymore."

"Don't trust the Winn." Her eyelids fluttered. "They will give you what they promise, but there will be unexpected consequences." She sighed. "They promise nothing without ulterior motives."

"I know, Mum." Cork squeezed her hand. "I's can handle 'em. We're gonna be fine. Yer gonna be fine."

She shook her head and inhaled, a harsh wheeze. "Don't do this for me, dear. I have accepted my fate."

"No!" Cork roared. It was maddening how his mother refused to fight for herself, to stay alive. "I'm doin' this. And I ain't never acceptin' yer fate."

"Kirth's will be done." His mother closed her eyes and soon fell back into snoring.

"Kirth be damned," Cork muttered.

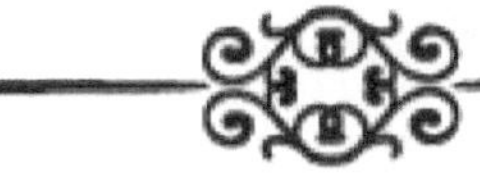

Arabella must have noticed Cork's foul mood when he returned to the carriage, because she immediately asked him what was wrong. She sat primly in the carriage across from a sleeping Nessa.

"Nothin'," Cork spat. He climbed into the carriage and rapped the side. "Let's go then," he yelled to the coachman.

Arabella sniffed dramatically. "Nothing rarely makes one such a black cloud of emotion."

"I ain't bleedin' emotional," he snapped.

Arabella gave him a supercilious smirk. "Clearly not. Did you complete Meldred's task?"

Cork nodded.

"And it was gloriously exciting and fulfilling."

Cork closed his eyes.

"Lovely chatting with you."

Cork pretended to snore.

The carriage made its way up the roads along Torr's River toward Ila on what promised to be a week's worth of being stuffed in a carriage with little to do but sleep or bicker.

Cork sat scrunched against the wall of the carriage, knees bent at a steep angle, pressed against the seat across from him where Arabella sat. There was no way for Cork to not touch her. His knees dug into her legs, but he kept his arms in his lap to avoid impeding on Nessa's space. Hopefully, whatever inn they found would be more comfortable.

To Cork's shock, Arabella had not complained about the cramped quarters and had made no remarks about Cork invading her side of the carriage. Nessa, however? Best to avoid her altogether. If he accidentally touched her, she might knife him.

Cork would have rather been on horseback, feeling the open air against his skin, but instead he sat, like a gods-damned gentleman, the black of his frock coat blending in with the dark wood of the carriage walls. Before they left Kilnic, the coachman had picked up another traveler, who now sat next to Cork. A bearded toff, hair finely coiffed in a curly mane: the latest style. Sweat pooled on the man's brow, and he smelled of souring perfume. The scent enveloped the stuffy carriage, and Cork had to open the carriage door and lean out into the brisk coastal air.

The man leaned out as well, pressing against Cork and peering out the window, huffing in Cork's ear each time the carriage bumped.

"Mind if I sit back down?" Cork brushed the man back into his seat. The man huffed once again.

Arabella seemed at ease, reading a leather-bound book entitled *The Lady and the Scoundrel*, all the while stroking a small white feather absentmindedly.

Cork picked at the sleeve of his frock coat. Meldred had assured him it was cut in the finest Rosenfellian tradition.

Looks like a coat to me.

It covered his forearms, though, so he didn't have to an-swer questions about his Dreamshapes, but the woolen coat scratched at his skin and was too kirthdamned warm for a carriage.

Nessa looked just as uncomfortable in the elegant black frock she wore, though she kept her cloak draped over her bare arms. Swordsman knew what Meldred had offered Nessa to get her to agree to dressing like a lady.

Cork looked out on the passing terrain. Craggy cliffs, the Sea of Dread on the other side of the cliffs, sparking blues and greens, a glittery sheen hiding the dangers within. The cliff sides adorned with yorn trees, thin-trunked and barely taller than Cork, but blooming with verdant greens and yellows.

Pity about the stench. Yorn trees smelled worse than refuse trenches, but gods, they were beautiful.

The surrounding ground had a thin layer of ice, glistening in the two suns, giving the coastline a vibrant sheen, as if it were alive.

And within a week, it would all be dead.

"Shame about the winter," the man said, stroking his beard in thought.

"Hmmm." Gods, the last thing Cork needed was more conversation. If the man got Arabella talking, there'd be no peace for the rest of the journey. Though then Nessa might stab them all. At least then it would be quiet.

The man pressed on, undeterred by Cork's lack of enthusiasm. "I mean to say, it's a pity all this beauty will freeze."

"Ya." Cork regarded the man with a brief glance before returning his attention to the view.

"Have you been to Frozen Lands before?" The toff drummed his fingers against the side of the carriage. "I've heard it's quite dangerous."

"No."

"I hope we won't find trouble on our way through."

Cork turned and grinned. "If we do, I'll make sure to bury yer body real nice-like."

The man sniffed and turned away, continuing to tap his fingers against the carriage door. Cork noticed Nessa smiling at him, a vicious sneer of a smile, but a sign she did have emotions beyond anger.

They spent the next hour in silence before stopping at an inn for lunch—a decent fish chowder and crusts of bread. The toff went to eat in a private back room with finer food and drink, no doubt. Nessa sat alone, but Arabella sat across from Cork. She remained suspiciously silent, but Cork caught her watching him in between bites, focusing especially on his arms—and the Dreamscapes underneath the coat.

"I can show 'em to you, if ya like."

Arabella choked on a bite of chowder. "That...that won't be necessary." Her face bloomed a light pink, and she turned away to cough.

"Just let me know. I can even flex my muscles a bit fer ya."

"This is quite excellent soup, is it not, Connick?" Arabella turned to Nessa. "Nessa, dear, don't you find the soup just divine?" Nessa glared daggers at her. "Well, I must find a privy before we continue our journey." Arabella stood and hurried from the room.

After enjoying a mug of ale—and the silence—it was time to return to the cramped carriage. Their erstwhile companion did not return, so Cork had more room to stretch his legs. He turned to the side and propped his legs up onto the seat.

Thank the Swordsman. Another day stuck in close quarters with that idiot, and I may have introduced him to my axe.

As the carriage passed along the coastline, past a thick, piney wood, Arabella called a meeting to order. She sat with her hands folded primly in her lap, her entire demeanor demure and ladylike as they discussed how to murder dozens of people.

"We need to figure out how we're going to do this," Arabella began.

Nessa lay propped against the carriage door, eyes closed. Not asleep, though. Cork expected she was lying in wait for the perfect moment to strike. Assassins like her didn't sleep.

Cork gave Arabella a steely glare. "We take axes. We use those axes." He nodded to Nessa. "Or daggers. Maybe even arrows." A convoluted strategy wasn't necessary for a job like this. They just needed to get to the Frozen Lands, find the Kirthed convoy, and do what they were getting paid for.

Arabella crossed her arms. "That's not good enough." Her lips trembled.

Ah, so she's nervous. Good. "It's all yer going to get."

Arabella began to rise, then hit her head on the ceiling of the carriage. "Shit." She slunk down like a wounded cat, hands on her knees, sulking. She glared at Cork. "Could you stop being so damned surly? I'm trying to be helpful, to add something to this job. The two of you may be seasoned warriors, killers even, but I'm not." Arabella paused, taking a breath to calm herself. She ran a hand over her face, rubbing her eyes to stave off tears. "And you, you both act like you despise me, and I've done absolutely nothing to deserve that. I've been kind, I've been pleasant, I've been a perfect bloody lady, and you still act like I'm beneath you."

Cork kept his glare on her. "Ya done?"

"No," Arabella put her head in her hands.

"Ya seem done." Cork cracked his knuckles. Another small smile from Nessa, even if she kept her eyes closed. "The reason we ain't making a plan is that things always go to shit. We could spend hours plannin', but then as soon as we get there, combat starts, people start dying. All those plans disappear. It's about survival at that point. We go to Ellid, wait at the inn for the forward party, follow 'em back to the convoy, and burn it to the ground. Kill anyone ya see. I'll keep one of 'em alive."

"But—"

Cork gave a smirk. "What did Meldred tell ya?"

"I'm not sure what you mean," Arabella said, looking out the window to avoid Cork's eyes.

"Yer supposed to listen to me." Cork pointed to his chest with his forefinger. "Follow my lead."

"But—"

"Shut up, girl," Nessa said. "Or I'll cut your tongue out."

Cork turned to see Nessa had finally opened her eyes. "Ah, yer awake."

Arabella threw her arms out, her hand hitting the carriage wall. She winced, then shook off the pain. "I don't know why you dislike me so much, but I haven't done anything to you." Her voice echoed in the tight carriage quarters.

"You exist, your ladyship." Nessa turned away and closed her eyes.

"You should consider your words." Arabella turned up her nose and crossed her arms. "Meldred wouldn't like it if he knew how you're treating me."

Nessa drew her dagger.

"Kirth me in the bollocks with a hot poker," Cork roared. "Put yer godsdamn dagger away."

Nessa eyed him, as if deciding whether to listen or slit Arabella's throat. Cork wished he had his axe within reach. Instead, it was with the luggage on the top of the carriage. He had a hunting knife, but he was no match for Nessa and her daggers if she decided to end the job and cut her losses, killing Arabella and himself.

Nessa's eyes flitted between her dagger, Arabella, and Cork. Cork clenched his jaw to the point of pain, waiting for Nessa to strike. Finally, Nessa grunted and put her dagger back into her boot.

Arabella let out a long, heavy breath. She'd most likely assumed her death was imminent as well. "That was absolutely unnecessary."

"Shut up," Cork snapped. "Ya ain't a lady here."

"Don't be silly, of course I'm a lady."

"Yer father's a cobbler, remember?"

"Oh Connick, being a lady is a state of mind." Arabella tipped an imaginary hat to Cork.

"Enough." Cork looked at each woman in turn. "Look, yer part of a team. And ya listen to what I say. Here's the bleedin' deal. We don't kill each other. We don't threaten each other either. Ya can hate me if ya like, and ya can go home and complain all about it to Meldred. When the job is done. For now, we put our personal feelings aside, and we go kill some people. Understood?"

"Understood," Arabella said in a muted voice. Nessa gave an almost imperceptible nod.

"Nessa?" Cork asked. He needed to hear her say it.

"Understood." Nessa opened her eyes. Cork stared into their depths, seeing nothing but seas of hatred.

Kirth, it would be a long carriage ride.

The next three days passed in a haze of cramped legs and conversations about nothing at all. Hours in the carriage, meals at taverns, inns, or a kind farmer's house, and very little conflict.

Nessa kept to herself, though Cork often caught her staring at him, eyes still blazing with hatred. For the best, Cork decided. If she needed to act on her anger, Nessa could go stab trees in the forest and pretend they were him. Just as long as she didn't jeopardize the job.

Arabella, however, had become an excellent traveling companion. She helped with unloading supplies at the inns and offered to do small tasks to help Cork, such as polishing his armor while he took a bath at one of the inns. His armor was fine the way it was, but he had to admit he enjoyed the sheen of the cuirass after a fresh polish. She'd even mended a small tear in his chainmail, a gift from an overzealous Kosellan raider a year back who'd had a mage-forged blade. It cut right through the mail and into Cork's side but thankfully missed his vital organs.

Cork didn't know much about women, but he wondered if he'd hit upon something that would help him keep order. Arabella had argued and whined whenever Cork had stayed mostly silent, but as soon as he'd begun to talk, to explain himself, she'd become much easier to deal with. Perhaps women appreciated a man who communicated? Communication was exhausting. Cork would rather stand naked in the Frozen Lands, armed with only a wooden sword, fighting off two hundred raiders. However, if it kept the job moving smoothly, then communicate he would.

Sleep was hard to come by sitting up in a carriage, but Cork lost consciousness now and then, while Nessa seemed to be in a near-constant state of sleep, though Cork assumed she was always watching. Arabella prattled away, and Cork did his best to respond with more than grunts, but after a while, he closed his eyes and hoped Arabella would cease talking.

They stopped at a tavern in Turnosis, a small farming community that was inhabited mostly by geese. The crooked path to the stone and thatch tavern was covered in the white beasts, flapping their wings and squawking at Cork as he dared intrude on their sanctum on his way to the tavern door.

"Filthy buggers," Cork muttered.

"I think they're adorable," Arabella said from his side. She strode past him and stepped too close to a particularly angry goose, who pecked at her legs. "Kirth!" Arabella hastily retreated behind Cork.

"Adorable." Cork grinned.

"Hmmph.'" Arabella pursed her lips, eyes lowering to the stone path. "Do you know why we're killing these people, Connick?"

The abrupt change of subject made Cork clench his shoulders. Yes, he knew why. Because the Winn had said it must be done. And because he needed tonic for his mother. "Not particularly." He shrugged. "Sometimes people need killin', and they hire us."

Arabella pulled at the folds of her skirt. "I just wonder—oh, it's silly of me—but I wonder about our victims. Their children and loved ones waiting for them at home."

"Yep, worst part of the job." Cork scratched at his nose. "Helps to just not think about it."

"It's beastly."

"Most things are."

"Why do you do this, Connick?" Her voice wavered. "The job."

Cork thought of his mother's sores. The blood. And the tonic she needed more than anything else. But he couldn't tell Arabella that. "Money, innit? Only godsdamn reason to do anything."

When they arrived at the Ellid inn, their final destination until the actual attack, things looked odd. Several horses tied to the posts outside, the front door wide open, the interior dark. Silence, other than the horses whinnying and stomping in place. It was midafternoon, but the suns were encased in a blanket of clouds.

"Quiet," Nessa said. She'd been in her sleep-like state for hours but now looked wide awake. "Strange."

"Why?" Arabella pursed her eyebrows in concern. "Inns are often quiet."

Nessa peered at Arabella. "Not with that many horses out front."

Cork exited the carriage and looked for signs of life. He heard someone speaking in low tones from behind the inn. A muffled scream.

"We's got trouble," he called back to the carriage. He threw off the frock coat, gathered his axe, and ran.

When he rounded the corner, Cork froze for a moment. Two men, dressed in faded leather breeches and jerkins, held a blonde woman by the shoulders, dunking her head in a horse trough.

"Don't you ever do that again," one man yelled as the woman struggled against her captors. "Any more mistakes, and you'll die."

"You should take your own advice," Cork said, advancing.

The men released the woman, who fell to the ground, gasping for air. They unsheathed swords and daggers and moved into fighting stances.

Cork circled them, waiting for either to make a move. As soon as one of them stepped forward to strike, Cork would counter with a heave of the axe, swinging it into the men. They'd probably block that first blow, but it would knock them off balance, and then Cork would set to work.

"Come on," Cork taunted. The men did not take the bait. Someone had trained them well enough to know that you should never step into the path of a huge weapon unless you knew you'd get by the blade. If the men rushed Cork, they'd have him at their mercy. However, they'd have to get past his blade first. If one of them was willing to sacrifice himself while the other struck, they'd have a good chance of defeating him.

Luckily for him, men like this, thugs and brigands, usually weren't willing to sacrifice themselves for their brethren.

And so, the men stayed back. Waiting.

Unfortunately for them, they waited long enough for Nessa to arrive.

Nessa? Didn't expect that.

Cork pushed the thoughts from his mind as one of the men, eyes wide in fear at the sight of Nessa charging, swung a heavy cut toward his shoulder. Cork moved his axe to block the man's strike with ease.

Nessa, daggers raised, vaulted through the air at the first man, who raised his sword to block her strike. Cork heaved his axe at the remaining foe; this time, his blade struck flesh, cutting deep into the man's shoulder, grinding against bone.

Cork heard the man's screams and gloried in it. Gods, it felt good. The man fell to his knees, and Cork gave him a boot to the face.

Nessa landed on top of her opponent, and they fell to the ground in a heap. He tried to lift his sword toward Nessa, but she was too fast. She rose to one knee, plunging a dagger into his throat, tearing it across an artery, spraying blood into her face. As the man coughed out his last strangled gasps, Nessa stood.

Cork moved to the wounded man, preparing to question him. What had the woman done that made them so angry? And who in Kirth were they? He reached down to lift the whimpering man up off of the ground, but Nessa was faster.

She sunk her dagger through the man's eye socket. Blood spurted onto Cork's face. He released the man, and the body crumpled to the ground.

Wiping the blood away, Cork fixed a glare on Nessa. "Godsdammit, I was gonna question him."

Nessa searched the man's pockets as if Cork hadn't spoken. Cork gripped his axe to the point his fingers turned white. This kirthdamned woman refused to follow directions. She acted without thought for anyone but herself. And worst of all, Cork understood why.

The feel of battle called to him. His axe had tasted blood, and he wanted more. To bring his blade down through the neck of the man, severing his head. He wanted blood, death, carnage.

Yet he'd restrained himself. For the good of everyone involved. Killing a thug did nothing beyond soak the ground with blood. If these men were part of a group, they clearly weren't the leaders. More would be coming when they didn't return.

Which meant Cork could either leave the inn behind and let the woman and her family deal with the repercussions or he could stay and deal with the consequences himself. As easy as it would be to run off into the Frozen Lands, Cork knew it wasn't an option.

Not when the Winn had ordered him to stay there.

Cork inhaled, then blew out a long breath, calming himself. "Nessa," Cork said. "That was stupid."

"Hmmph," Nessa said, still looting.

Cork sheathed his axe. "I was gonna question 'em." He scanned the mud-soaked area, but the woman was gone. A glint of red caught Cork's eye. Arabella, peeking around the corner of the inn, watching, her face paler than the Frozen Lands. She caught Cork's eye, then disappeared from view.

Nessa shrugged. "They deserved it."

"It doesn't matter if they deserved it. It was stupid. Now we don't know why they were here."

"I don't give a shit about that," Nessa said. "They're dead. Now we move on."

"We can't move on. This buggerin' inn's our kirth-damned destination."

"Not my issue." Nessa stood and dusted off her knees. "You're welcome for the assistance."

"Why did ya help? Ya act like ya can't be arsed to help anyone unless yer paid." He gestured to the peeling paint on the inn's exterior. "Well, I doubt lawyone in this shithole has any intention of payin' ya."

Nessa regarded him with a cold stare. "I was bored. Been stuck with you lot for days on end now, and this was something to do. Something to get me away from milady Arabella." She stalked back toward the carriage.

Cork followed, cursing both women's names.

Arabella sat in the carriage, hands folded primly, an unconcerned air about her. Her face was still a sickly white, though.

"Thanks for your assistance," Cork grumbled. He rolled up the bloodstained sleeves of his shirt, exposing his Dreamshapes.

"You're quite welcome," Arabella said. "I, erm, assumed you wouldn't wish all our supplies to sit unattended." She relaxed her shoulders, pointing to the crates of food and extra weapons on the floor of the carriage.

Cork crossed his arms and furrowed his brow. "Supplies won't matter if we're dead."

"You seem quite alive to me." Arabella gave a coy smile. "Angry, but alive."

Cork glared at her. He couldn't decide which of the two women in his company was more frustrating: Nessa, who killed whoever she came across, or Arabella, who acted like it was all a game.

"Swordsman's tears," Cork cursed. He turned away and walked to the inn. Anything to get a moment's peace.

The inn was cozier than expected, considering the crumbling exterior. A fire roared in the hearth at the back of the main hall, warming a seating area with several velvet-upholstered cushioned chairs. There was a bar top with four stools, and three wooden tables were arranged in the middle of the room. The floors were sawdust, but a clean sawdust. No sign of spilled food, vomit, feces, or blood, unlike most of the establishments Cork found along the road.

Two men sat at the bar, drinking whiskey and talking quietly. Behind the bar top stood the woman who'd been out back not long before, head in a horse trough. Her hair was wet still, but she wiped the bar with a cloth as if she'd not been on the verge of unconsciousness or death not fifteen minutes before.

Cork walked up to the woman and sat at the bar.

"What can I get you, sir?" The woman's eyes flitted toward Cork's face before moving away, as if she was afraid to look at him.

"My throat's dry. Need somethin' to wet it." Cork gave her a meaningful look. "And all the water around here has been used recently. Don't wish to drink what's just been used to wash someone's hair."

"Of course, sir." The woman still refused to meet his eye. "I have ale and whiskey."

Turnos' tits. "Look here," Cork said, taking a gruff tone. "You and I both know that not long ago, ya were being drowned behind the inn. What in the Swordsman's name was happening? Why were those men doing that to ya?"

"It don't concern you," the woman said.

"Two men are dead behind your godsdamned inn," Cork said. "I'd say it concerns me."

Nessa entered the inn, empty-handed other than her daggers, while Arabella carried a crate of food. Cork sighed. Leaving most of the work for him as usual.

"I can't say nothin'." The woman bit her lip, and Cork thought he saw her face tremble. "They'll kill all of us. Not just me. Everyone in town. I thank you for what you did, but I can't talk about it."

"Do you know Meldred?" Cork asked. The woman looked at him, confused, and shook her head. "He's a friend of mine. A powerful friend. He mentioned having associates in the area. They might be able to help you."

"I've not heard that name."

Cork decided to try a different tactic. "What about any strange folk about?"

"Only you and your friends."

Cork smirked. "Stranger than us by half. Walkin' 'round as if in a trance, probably dressed all in black."

"Those Winn buggers? Aye, they're all 'round these parts."

Kirth, Cork hadn't expected that. The Winn were usually better at staying out of sight. Apparently, they wanted to be seen.

"Ah, where would I be able to find 'em?" Cork gave her his biggest, most innocent smile.

The woman's gaze drifted to Cork's Dreamshapes. "Yer one of 'em, ain't ya?"

"Not anymore."

The woman's eyes flicked toward two men at the bar. "I dunno, but those fellers there might know. Saw 'em out front talking to the Winn yesterday." The woman absentmindedly wiped glasses with a rag. Her shoulders were as tight as a bowstring, fear burning in her eyes. What was so terrifying? Those men or the Winn?

Cork eyed the men at the bar. "Do you know those men? They're locals?"

"No, seen 'em once or twice here getting a drink, but haven't spoke to 'em. They keep to themselves." She brushed a hand against her sodden hair. "But I know who they work for."

"I'll have wee chat with them, then."

The woman shook her head violently. "No, they'll kill me."

"Ain't gonna talk about you," Cork said. "Figured I'd just try to make a new friend, eh?"

"Bugger you all." The woman retreated into the back room, leaving the bar unattended.

Might as well ease my thirst. Cork grabbed a jug of ale from the counter and filled a large tankard. *Figure I've earned this.*

Before heading over to introduce himself to the two men, Cork went out to the carriage to unload his supplies. No point in leaving them outside to be scavenged by any wandering thieves.

Arabella awaited him outside the inn, arms crossed. "I heard what the innkeeper said. We need to do something to help."

Cork sighed. "Not now." He brushed past her to the carriage. A door slammed behind him. Arabella wasn't going to help carry anything, then.

After unloading everything and bidding farewell to the coachman, Cork lugged the crates into the inn. Arabella had retrieved the innkeeper and booked two rooms. One for him and the other for her and Nessa.

They'll be pleasant bunkmates.

Once Cork had carried the luggage up to the rooms, he and a red-faced Arabella returned to the main hall of the inn. Nessa stayed in her room, telling them that she was "shittin' tired and tired of the both of you shits."

At the door to the main hall, Cork stopped. "Wait. You stay here and keep watch."

Arabella stomped a foot. "But—"

"Stay here."

"Of course," Arabella scoffed, rolling her eyes. "I shall stand in the drafty hallway while you enjoy sitting down for a drink."

In response, Cork grunted once more and made his way into the room. He moved to the bar and pulled up a chair next to the two men, who looked up at him with annoyed glares.

"Wot d'ya want?" one of the men asked. He had several days worth of stubble hanging off his stringy neck and looked more like a turkey than a man. "We're busy-like."

"Just wanted to invite the two of ya over for a drink," Cork said. "I'm having' a celebration of sorts. Figured you looked like men who wouldn't turn down a free mug of ale."

The two men exchanged glances. "Bugger off," the turkey man said.

His companion, a short, squat man with a forgettable face, bared his brown teeth at Cork. "Like he says. Piss off."

Cork crossed his arms. "If ya talk to me like that, we're gonna have a problem." He glanced at his Dreamshapes and back at the men, hoping they'd take the hint. He was a big, bad, Winn monster who would kill them, eat their children, and let his wolvinn mounts piss on their graves. They should not trifle with him.

"You don't scare us, ya Winn bastard," Turkey-man said. "We've got friends, see. Powerful friends. And they say what's allowed and what isn't here in Ellid. So like I said. Bugger off before we slit yer throat."

Cork smiled. "My apologies. Didn't mean no harm, did I?" He bowed and returned to Arabella.

"You didn't axe them," Arabella tugged at her ear.

"Not yet." Cork smirked. It would have been easy to pull out his axe and kill the bastards, but it wouldn't get him closer to finding the Winn. In fact, it would only make things worse. "But they did tell me they's got powerful friends."

"Ah," Arabella said. "So we find the powerful friends and axe them."

Cork shook his head. "No."

Arabella froze, mouth falling open. "What?"

"We's don't got time. If we wasn't on a job already, I'd say sure, let's help the people. But now? We's gotta focus on the job."

Arabella blinked rapidly. "But they'll die."

"Yeah." Cork wanted to take Arabella's hand, to tell her it would all be all right. He stared into her hazel eyes, sparkling with innocence, and felt a powerful urge to...protect her? Her insouciant mask had fallen away, revealing the confused young woman beneath it.

He could lie to her. But things wouldn't be all right. There was nothing they could do for the people of Ellid.

"It's monstrous."

"Most things are."

Arabella turned away from him, looking up the stairs toward their chambers. "I can't believe you would abandon an entire town."

"I don't want to." Cork bit down on the inside of his lip. "But we's got to do the job."

Arabella swung back around, arms crossed. "Kirth take the job."

"No," Cork bit out. His mind flashed back to his mother, the sores, the blood. How weak she looked, how she could barely stand sometimes. "Shut the hell up, woman."

Arabella recoiled as if Cork had struck her. "Well, umm, maybe Nessa will help me." She raced up the stairs.

Cork laughed at that. "She hates you more than me," he called after her.

"Yes, but I'm more persuasive than you." Arabella stopped at the top of the stairs. "And I have some money saved that might speak to her baser instincts." Arabella disappeared into her chambers, slamming the door behind her.

"Good luck with that," Cork muttered. He returned to the bar, nodding to the two men. They rose, one of them spitting on the floor, and hastily exited the inn.

Cork grinned and lifted the jug of ale. "How's bout another round?"

After a few minutes, Arabella returned, eyes red and cheeks blotchy. She flung herself down into the chair next to Cork and poured herself a large glass of ale, which she downed in one gulp.

"Nessa said no, then?"

"I don't wish to talk about it." Arabella stared blankly at her hands on the counter in front of her.

They sat in silence for a few minutes, something Cork gloried in. But then he felt a pang of something in his gut.

It was odd. He didn't like seeing Arabella upset, even if he didn't want her prattling away either.

Finally, Arabella broke the silence. "Well, if you won't help, I'll do it myself." She stood, pushed the chair roughly against the bar, and headed for the inn door.

"What are ya—"

"I'm saving the town, Cork. Since no one else will." Arabella opened the door and was gone.

Shit. The last thing Cork could afford was Arabella ruining the job by causing trouble in town and either getting captured or killed. Cork stood with a sigh, finished the jug of ale, and headed after her.

When Cork reached the courtyard, Arabella was nowhere to be seen. Nothing to do but head into town. Ellid wasn't much to look at. Stables, a few farms, and a collection of ramshackle wooden huts near the edge of town. There couldn't be more than a hundred residents. There'd be nowhere for them to sleep. Cork wandered the main thoroughfare, if you could call it that, searching for signs of life. The cool air pricked at his face, and everything smelled vaguely of manure.

To the north, outside of the town, a sizable manor house sat in mild disrepair. It needed a fresh coat of paint, but the window shutters looked new. Green and white, with a touch of red from the thatched roof. Probably the headquarters of the powerful friends of the men at the inn.

And the place Cork needed to keep Arabella away from. The last thing they needed now was to take on the entire criminal underworld of Ellid.

A flash of movement to Cork's left brought him out of his thoughts. Arabella strode toward him, face still flushed from crying, her mouth turned up in a sneer. "I thought you weren't going to help me."

"I'm not. Gotta make sure ya don't die, girl."

Arabella huffed. "I'm quite capable of taking care of myself."

"Capable of dyin', at least."

"Hardly." Arabella gave him a withering look.

"What're ya planning to do now that yer here?"

Arabella gestured to the shops around them, which were little more than shacks. "I was preparing to interrogate the locals. Ask them what they knew about those ne'er-do-wells terrorizing their town."

"Ah."

Cork's lack of faith in her plan must have shown because she swatted at the folds of her tunic and glared at him. "If you're quite done with your insults, you may leave. I have things well under control here."

Cork laughed. "Aye, so that's why ya went runnin' off into town, drippin' tears, and moanin' about how ya didn't get yer way. 'Cause ya had things under control." He sneered wickedly. "What did Nessa say to ya, then?"

"What do you mean?" Arabella reached a hand up to her face to hide her blushes.

"You've been broodin' and stompin' about ever since ya came back from talkin' to her. Specially since ya tried to get her to come with ya." Cork gestured to the emptiness around them. "And she ain't here."

"She said she wanted to knife me," Arabella said in little more than a whisper. She pulled at the sleeves of her dress, fighting off shivers. "Said she'd kill me first chance she got."

Cork reached out to put a hand on her shoulder but stopped just as he was about to touch her. Normally, he'd pat a coworker on the back and tell 'em they'd drink the pain away later. What did you say to a damned lady, though? Gods, if he patted her on the back, she might topple over.

"What are you doing, Connick?" Arabella stared at his hand, which still hovered just above her shoulder.

Bugger. Cork withdrew his hand and shuffled his feet awkwardly. This damned woman always made him anxious. "Ya want to ask questions? It'll be dusk soon. Reckon we'd better get to askin' questions."

"I do appreciate your approval." Arabella's lips curled slightly, ever sardonic. "And thank you, Connick. You might be a great bore sometimes, but you're not so bad underneath it all."

Cork's stomach fluttered; he couldn't help but grin.

The first two shops, a tanner's workshop and weapon-smith, seemed abandoned and on the verge of collapse. Cork knocked, but no one answered. The third shop didn't appear to sell anything at all—the shelves were bare, and there was no sign out front. An old, wrinkled woman shook her head at their questions but said nothing.

Finally, in the fourth shop, they had luck. A lamp burned in the window of the small cobbler's shop, the air filled with the distinct clanging of hammers against nails.

"Let me handle this," Arabella said, stepping forward to the door. "I know the cobbler life."

"Travelin' across the nation to escape the cobbler life, and here the gods bring ya right back to it." Cork winked at her, and Arabella's face flushed again. Kirth, was he flirting with her?

"I'll never escape, it seems." Arabella rapped her knuckles against the door. "Oh well. I'll always have stylish shoes."

The interior of the cobbler shop smelled of leather, sweat, and a tangy sweetness Cork couldn't place. A one-room shop filled to the brim with shoes in various states of construction. The cobbler, a wispy, balding man clad in faded black linen, looked up from a pair of black leather riding boots and nodded to Arabella. Cork did his best to fade into the background of the shop, even as the top of his head almost reached the low-hanging roof of the shack.

"What can I do for you, miss?" The cobbler asked.

"Oh, it's so lovely to see you," Arabella said, smiling widely as if talking to a friend.

The cobbler's eyes moved to Cork and then back to Arabella. "Do we know each other, miss?"

"I feel as if we do." Arabella moved forward and wrapped the cobbler in an enormous hug.

The cobbler staggered back, as if he'd been struck. "I assure you, miss, this is an honorable shop. My wife—"

"Oh, don't be silly," Arabella chided, crossing her arms. "I'm not here to seduce you. I'm just so happy to meet a fellow cobbler."

The cobbler looked her up and down, eyes squinted in confusion. "Cobblers don't usually carry weapons."

Arabella tapped her bow. "Well, I'm other things as well. If you've been to Kilnic, you might have heard of my father's shop. Howston and Sons." She rolled her eyes. "I'm sons."

The cobbler's posture relaxed. "Aye, I've heard of Howstons. Fine shop from what I've been told."

Arabella favored him with a polite nod of thanks. "It's lovely to hear that. My father has often told me of the fine craftsmen in Ellid as well." She paused and gestured to Cork. "The reason my, well, my husband and I are here today is to get information." She winked. Cork's face burned. Gods, he was probably blushing now. *Bloody Arabella. Winking is my thing, damn it.*

"My apologies, sir," the cobbler said to Cork. "I didn't mean to imply anything untoward about your wife—"

Cork grunted. He wasn't sure he could speak actual words just then. Arabella was right there, a beaming smile on her face, looking beautiful and self-assured, and Cork just felt embarrassed. Embarrassed to be standing there, the topic of conversation. Or embarrassed because he didn't entirely hate the idea of Arabella and him together. Not married. Kirth, no. Cork would lose his godsdamned mind if he spent more than a few more weeks with her. But a bit of fun on the job? Cork fought to keep the smile from his face. He'd be up for that. Usually. Not this job, though.

"Darling, are you quite all right?" Arabella's voice broke into Cork's thought. He realized he'd been standing there, eyes closed, silent, even though the cobbler had addressed him.

"Fine," Cork ground out.

Arabella shook her head playfully at the cobbler. "My husband is not much of a conversationalist, I fear. But he's quite good with that axe. The only protection a lady needs." She placed one hand on her hip. "But back to the information we need. I know how we cobblers keep our noses to the ground. People tell us things while we're fixing up their finest pair of boots."

"Aye."

"Well, we're looking for information about a group of powerful individuals in the area."

The cobbler swallowed and gave a shiver. "I've got nothing to say."

"I won't tell a soul, I swear."

The cobbler shook his head, glancing at Cork, who narrowed his eyes and gave him his best *talk-and-I'll-axe-you* glare. "Like I said, I've got nothing to say." The cobbler focused his eyes on the floor. "I'd be happy to sell you some shoes, though."

"Thanks ever so much," Arabella said, placing an arm on the cobbler's shoulder. "We appreciate you."

"Anyone else odd about?" Cork asked. "Not about the buggers ya don't want to talk about," he added, noticing the cobbler's fearful expression. "I mean outsiders." Cork rubbed the Dreamshapes on his left arm. "Foreigners, even."

"No, sir, I haven't seen anyone odd like that. Except you, of course, begging your pardon."

"My husband is a good man." Arabella glared daggers at the cobbler. "And really quite vicious with his axe."

"Of course, miss, I didn't mean anything by it."

"Well, we'll be leaving now." Arabella eyed the boots the cobbler had been working on. "But, when you finish those fine leather boots, I'll certainly come back for a look."

When they'd left the cobbler shop, Arabella stopped in Cork's path and peered up at him, lips pursed in thought. "Why do you keep asking about odd people?"

"What?"

"You've asked our cobbler friend about odd foreigners, and I heard you ask those men at the inn a similar question." Arabella placed a finger against Cork's chest. "You're hiding something from me."

Cork grinned slyly. "I'm hidin' a lot of things from ya. Wouldn't want to offend ya, yer ladyship, with my hard ways."

"Oh, come off it." Arabella poked her finger harder. If Cork hadn't been wearing armor, he may have ended up with a bruise. "You're lying to me. About the job."

Cork brushed past her, moving toward the outskirts of town. "Ain't got nothin' else to say."

"Cork!" Arabella's raised voice echoed throughout the town. "Get back here and talk to me, now!"

"Yes, ma'am." Cork continued to walk away, heading toward a forested area off the path back to the inn.

The first sign of the Winn wouldn't have been obvious to anyone other than Cork. Pools of ice, mostly crushed, the remnants of a Winn ice hammer. Either there'd been a battle here—unlikely considering the lack of blood—or the Winn had been practicing their magic.

Cork kicked at the ice. Still mostly frozen. Couldn't have been long.

"What in Kirth's name?" Arabella asked, stepping up beside him.

"Ice, innit?" Cork turned a corner of the path and caught a flash of movement from behind a large tree. "Got company," he said in a low voice. "Get yer bow out."

Arabella said nothing, but Cork heard the shuffling of arrows behind him. He pulled his axe from its sheath and stepped forward.

A massive creature stood in his path. A wolf, but larger by half, its maw dripping with blood as it ripped into a rabbit's carcass.

Arabella raised her bow to shoot.

"Wait." Cork raised a finger. "Give me a moment."

"What are you doing?" Arabella's voice was heavy with fear. "That monster's going to eat us!"

"Hello, girl," Cork said. He lowered his axe and stepped forward slowly, letting the wolf sniff at him. The wolf snorted and pawed at the rabbit carcass.

Cork reached out to the wolf's side and caressed it gently. "Yer a good girl, ain't ya?" His hand moved to the wolf's snout. The wolf opened its mouth, and, as Arabella shrieked in terror, it licked Cork's face, its scratchy tongue leaving blood streaks down Cork's cheek.

Arabella stared on, wide-eyed. "What?"

Cork looked back at Arabella as he scratched the wolf's snout. "It's a wolvinn, innit?"

"What the bloody Kirth is a wolvinn?"

Cork pointed at the panting wolvinn and patted her head. "Big wolf."

"I can see that," Arabella scoffed.

"Winn use 'em."

"Good gods, what are the Winn doing here?"

Cork sighed. "Well, probably causin' problems. That's what they normally do." He gestured toward the wolvinn. "You wanna give her a pet?"

Arabella went pale, as if the very idea made her nauseous. "I'll just...admire her from a distance."

A shrieking whistle came from nearby trees, and the wolvinn's ears shot up. From behind the trees came two familiar figures, clad in the dark robes of the Winn. The same Winn he'd met at the Cross. The ones who'd threatened his mother.

Cork cursed under his breath.

Trellen Winn gazed at Cork through unblinking eyes. "Corkelle Winn, all is well?"

Cork's heart sunk. Arabella would have even more questions now. "Aye."

"Wait, they know you?" Arabella watched on with an aghast expression.

"The Flock wonders if you are being loyal, Corkelle Winn," Yannel Winn said. "This is not the path you were hired to follow."

"The Flock can—" Cork took a deep breath. Anger wouldn't help anything. "Look, the convoy ain't here yet. I fancied a stroll."

"You have not been paid to meddle in local affairs, Corkelle Winn. Should you continue, there will be consequences." Trellen dropped his eyes demurely to the ground. "Your penance only increases."

Would you bugger off? Cork squeezed his hands together. Gods, he'd felt helpless too often lately. There was little he could do here, other than agree or directly disobey the Winn. And that would spell doom for his mother.

"I understand." Cork lowered his own eyes, hoping this was the correct thing to do. His mother hadn't taught him that many of the Winn customs. "I will, uhh, honor the Flock, like."

"Blessings," the Winn both chanted as one.

"Not to interrupt," Arabella said, stepping forward to stand next to Cork, "but I have no bloody idea what's happening." She looked at Cork and then at the Winn. "I thought Meldred hired us for this job?"

"Aye," Cork said. "He did. The Winn hired Meldred, and he gave the job to us."

"And they're following us around?"

"Well, the Winn are—" *Creepy buggers,* he wanted to say. Cork met the eyes of the taller Winn. "They're fond of makin' sure shit gets done right."

"Do not fail us, Corkelle Winn." With final, emotionless stares, the Winn departed into the trees, their flowing robes making it seem like they glided. The wolvinn trotted after her masters, and Cork felt a pang of something. Sadness? A desire to keep the wolvinn? He realized he didn't care at all if the Winn in the area died, but he desperately wanted that wolvinn to be okay.

Arabella also watched the wolvinn depart, though Cork wondered if she was glad to see it go. Perhaps she was still worried the wolvinn would eat her. "What do you know about the job? Things you haven't told me?"

Cork sighed. A conversation he'd hoped to avoid. "Won't hurt to tell ya now." Cork motioned to the tree where the wolvinn had been earlier. "Might as well sit. May take a while."

Cork told her the whole truth—how the Winn had hired them in secret and wanted them to destroy the convoy of their enemies—people who'd somehow defied Winn laws—and leave one survivor to report back the destruction. It wasn't simply destroying a convoy but acting in the service of a foreign nation. Depending on who they attacked, it could even be an act of war.

Afterward, Arabella seemed at a loss. Muted. She leaned against the tree and put her head in her hands, trembling. "I've never interacted with the Winn. Besides you, that is, and I know nothing of politics or nations at war. I just wanted to get out of Kilnic and do something." She moved her hands down to her lap and met Cork's eyes. "But I don't know if I can do it, Cork. In the city, it was all target practice. Shooting at inanimate objects, following my mother's directions."

"Well, yer the one who chose to be a mercenary."

"That first job was so easy. We rode horses, guarded our client, and drank ale. No combat." She looked at Cork for a moment before returning her eyes to the ground. "I don't know if I can kill someone in cold blood."

Cork spat over his shoulder. "I don't think yer cut out for this life, lass."

"I know." Arabella sighed. "I thought it would be an adventure. Not this."

Cork rubbed his brow, thinking. "Ya killed a man in Kilnic. A week ago."

Arabella considered this. "And I've been trying for days to pretend it never happened. I didn't see his eyes when I killed him."

"Ain't gonna see their eyes when you shoot 'em from a distance."

Arabella continued as if Cork hadn't spoken. "What will it be like when my target is right in front of me, begging me not to be shot?"

"Ya do what ya have to do. Hit the target."

Arabella gave a rueful laugh. "In Kilnic, my arrow was aimed toward a target. I hit that target. Just like my mother taught me. I didn't even see the impact. I'd already moved my attention toward you and the remaining men." She sighed and brought a hand to her temple, rubbing at it. "There was no sound. No anguished look." She inhaled deeply. "It's almost like it didn't happen. That's what I tell myself, at least. I try not to think about it all. I know they weren't good men, but taking a life? It's horrific."

"That's natural," Cork said. "Look, I've killed a lot of men in the past few years. Fought in two wars and taken on countless groups of highwaymen and raiders. It gets easier, but you never fully get used to it."

"Nessa seems to have."

"Normal people don't get used to it. Nessa is…" Cork trailed off.

"The opposite of normal."

"She's a killer."

"These people we're supposed to kill. Do we know anything about them? Are they villains or enemy soldiers? Or normal people? Like us."

"That's how the enemy usually is," Cork said. "They're just like you. They just follow the orders of someone who disagrees with your boss."

Arabella reached out and held Cork's arm, just below the shoulder, gripping harder than necessary. "How do you do it? Kill innocent people."

Cork shrugged. "I've got people I care about who need my help. And the money's good. If I don't have money, I can't help—" He faltered. "I can't help my mum."

Arabella placed her hand on Cork's cheek. Cork tensed but didn't move her hand away.

"Your mum?"

"She's sick. Happens with anyone who lives on the Isle for too long and then leaves. There's something about the mages there. I dunno if it's in the water or the food or an injection they give you, but Winn mages who leave the Isle for more than a year get sick. Starts with weakness, tiredness, losing weight. Then ya start coughing blood. You's can barely stand. Sores everywhere. Yer a godsdamn husk of a person."

"Can you do anything for her?" Arabella moved her hand down to Cork's arm, tracing his Dreamshapes with one finger.

"Take her back to the Isle. That'd cure her, but she refuses. So instead, I's buy tonics for her. Some of the mages in the city—the ones with Winn connections—sell them. Gives ya energy, eases the pain. Kirthed expensive and it don't last, but it eases the suffering for a bit at least."

"Oh gods, Cork—"

"It's why I took this job. Can't buy tonic without money."

"And if you have to kill people for that money?"

"It's worth it."

Arabella shuddered, exhaling deeply. "And I suppose that means we can't help the townspeople. It'll spell your mother's doom."

"Yep." Cork took Arabella's hand and gently removed it from his Dreamshapes. Right now, he needed to focus on the job.

"I wish we could just kill them. These men who are threatening the town. Help people, make a difference." Arabella smiled ruefully. "This mercenary life is more complicated than I thought it would be."

"I get it." Cork brushed grass from his trousers and got to his feet. He reached out a hand and helped Arabella stand as well. It was difficult to let go of her hand once more, but she gave his hand a slight squeeze and then extricated her hand from his grasp. "I like helpin' people. But right now, we've got to think about the job."

"Even when it's shit."

"Even when it's shit. Can't save everyone." Cork picked his axe up off the ground and sheathed it. "Sometimes innocent people die. And sometimes, even if it makes ya feel godsdamn miserable, ya can only save yourselves."

Arabella nodded. "And hopefully, your mother as well."

"That too. Come on, we's got an advance party to find and a convoy to destroy."

PART THREE:

EVERYTHING GOES TO SHIT

THE SUNS HAD ALMOST vanished when Cork and Arabella returned to the inn. Nessa stood out front, cloaked in black, barely visible in the dusky haze of Trunellic evening, carving a design into the inn door: a dagger with heavy marks through it, all harsh slashes and fraying wood.

"Yer not much of an artist," Cork said, squinting at the door.

Nessa scowled in response and turned to face them. "Where in Kirth have you been? The forward party is here. I was getting tired of waiting to kill them. Come on." Nessa swept into the inn. Arabella shook her head and swatted Cork on the shoulder as they followed Nessa.

In the corner of the inn near the hearth, a jovial bearded man sat with a young boy, no more than sixteen, and an armor-clad woman. The man and the boy were dressed in riding leathers, shortswords displayed prominently on their sides, while the woman wore armor and carried a longsword strapped to her back.

Kirth, they had a boy with them. Cork's stomach churned at the thought of bringing his axe down into the head of someone so young.

Cork attempted to move past them without attracting their attention, but before he made it halfway across the great hall, the bearded man gave him a hearty wave.

"Our deliverers!" the bearded man called out. "Please join us. You deserve an ale. Kirth, maybe a full barrel." He gave a deep, guttural laugh, and his companions smiled along with him.

"Yes, please come sit with us," the woman said in a thick accent Cork didn't recognize. She was middle-aged with graying hair and a leathery face—no doubt from years of traveling through the frigid conditions of the Frozen Lands. However, she had a kind smile, and Cork felt like, under different circumstances, he would have trusted her. Tightly muscled arms and an expensive-looking dark metal breastplate showed she was no stranger to a fight. Someone who would have been an excellent coworker.

However, she had to die.

"I'd hoped to avoid this," Cork muttered to Arabella.

"Well, just smile, and let me do the talking."

"I'd hoped to avoid that as well." Cork sighed. "Come on." They approached the group.

"Ales all around!" the bearded man bellowed to the innkeeper, who nodded her acknowledgment. "I'm Ruckels, and this is my son, Torsten." He pointed to the boy, who

Cork didn't think resembled Ruckels much. "This is our associate, Myrna." He pointed to the woman.

"I'm afraid you have us at a disadvantage," Arabella said, sitting down at the table. Cork followed suit. "While it's lovely to meet you, we're unclear what exactly we've delivered you from."

Ruckels frowned and looked past them to the bar, where the innkeeper stood, cleaning mugs. "Our lovely hostess told us of your brave deed, killing thugs and saving the inn. Quite the talker, that one."

"She said all that, did she?" Cork looked at the woman, who still refused to meet his eye. "Strange, she hasn't spoken much to me."

"Perhaps she's still just overwhelmed with gratitude," Myrna said with a sardonic gleam in her eyes.

"Must be," Cork grunted. "I'm Cork, and this is Arabella." No need for fake identities. No one here would have ever heard of them, except perhaps the Winn. "We're traveling east to Ila to visit family."

"Married?" Ruckels asked.

Cork swallowed. Best to avoid that topic again. The cobbler's shop had been awkward enough. "Ahem, no, not married." He and Arabella exchanged glances. Gods, she had a wry smile on her face. Enjoying his discomfort.

"Not yet, at least," Arabella took Cork's hand in hers. "That's why we're traveling to Ila. We need my father's blessing."

"Long way to travel, just the two of you," Myrna said. "Might end up more than just betrothed."

"Aye, get an early start on that family." Ruckels guffawed, slapping the table.

Arabella's face blushed crimson. "Oh, no, things are quite proper. We brought along a friend to act as our chaperone."

Cork had to fight back a laugh. The thought of Nessa being a friend was too ludicrous not to smile.

"More of a bodyguard than a friend," Cork said.

"And yet she ain't here." Myrna cocked her head. "Giving the young couple in love quite a bit of freedom, isn't she?"

"Cork's a perfect gentleman." Arabella squeezed Cork's arm reassuringly.

In response, Cork spat on the floor. "Aye, regular poncey noble, I am."

"And yet you seem to know your way around an axe," Ruckels said.

"Aye. But one axe won't do much against a horde. Three fighters is better than one."

"Three?"

"I know how to shoot," Arabella said. "Our dear innkeeper friend didn't witness it, but I'm an excellent shot."

"And quite humble, like," Cork said, squeezing her hand. Arabella's skin was soft and smooth, and Cork had to remind himself to move his hand away.

Ruckels smiled. No doubt he noticed Cork's lingering grasp. "Nothing like young lovers." He snorted and took a sip of ale. "Well, I'm mighty glad you decided to travel east to get your father's blessing. We could have fought off the thugs ourselves if need be, but it would have slowed us down." He shook his head. "Amazing how many brigands there are along this road."

Cork nodded. "Reckon they'd get too cold up here and rob people somewhere warmer, eh?"

"We've made this trip three times a year for the past decade. Never-ending supply of bandits in these parts." Ruckels quaffed some ale. "Course, it's keeps us in a job. What kind of work do you do, Cork?"

"Well, uh—"

"Cork fixes problems for those who can pay." Arabella placed her hands primly on the table. "He's quite helpful that way. And in some cases, as with our lovely innkeeper friend, he does it for free."

"Aye, I reckoned you were much like us," Myrna said. "We swing our blades for pay as well."

Ruckels nodded. "Got a convoy comin' up through these parts. With all the bandits along the roads here, our employers have tripled the protection."

"How many men do ya have?" Cork asked, trying to keep his voice even. "I haven't ever worked in a party of more than ten."

"Around that many, if you count our employers." Ruckels gestured to Myrna and Torsten. "I was sent ahead to scout out the terrain, deal with any brigands. Picked my team wisely. Myrna's our best fighter, and Torsten's good with a blade as well."

"Maybe better than you, old man." Torsten punched his father's arm good-naturedly.

Cork fought off a smile. Gods, he liked these people. In another situation, they'd be friends. Instead, tomorrow, he'd be killing them. "Must be important, this convoy."

"Aye, we're part of a supply convoy out of Oban. We've traveled up through Kosel and now across the Frozen Lands."

Oban made sense, considering Myrna's thick accent, but what would the Obanni have against the Winn? "Quite a long journey, that. A supply convoy," Cork said slowly. "Weapons, then?"

Ruckels narrowed his eyes. "Kirth, no. Supplies. Food, ale, furs. Medicine for the poor and downtrodden along the Sea of Dread."

Cork felt his heart pounding. He swallowed down the bile that threatened to rise up. Thank the gods Arabella was there.

"Ah, a worthy cause." Arabella shot Cork a look. Cork wanted to sink into the ground beneath him.

"Just know, you played a part in this, killing those bandits." Ruckels stood and squeezed Cork's arm. "The needy will have a hot meal and blankets to stave off the worst of the cold. You're a godsdamned hero."

"No," Cork snapped. "I'm just a man."

Buggering shit. Cork lay on the too-comfortable bed, gripping the sheets, breathing slowly as his stomach churned. Ruckels and his crew were normal people. Good people, even, on a mission of charity. What did the bleedin' Winn have against them? Maybe the Winn were as monstrous as everyone made them out to be.

However, Cork knew the convoy party had to die. It was either his mother or them, and there was only one choice there. The next morning, he'd do the job.

The door creaked open, and Arabella entered. Cork wore only a pair of linen undershorts, but he made no move to cover himself. She'd chosen to come into his bedchambers, after all.

Arabella's gaze strayed to Cork's stomach for a moment before she fixed her eyes on his. Through the faded light of the oil lamp, blotches of wetness shone on Arabella's cheeks, leaving a trail down her face from eye to chin. She wore a thin dress, and on another night, Cork would have enjoyed having an underdressed woman in his room. Tonight, though, a tumble in bed was the farthest thing from his mind.

"This whole situation is shit." Arabella leaned against a post at the foot of the bed.

"Aye."

"They're trying to help refugees, people with nothing. And we're just going to kill them? And then, when the supplies are destroyed, that means we're killing the refugees as well."

"Aye."

Arabella exhaled sharply. "Are you going to say anything other than bloody aye, Cork?"

"Nothin' else I say will change anything, will it?"

"I suppose not. If you won't help...maybe Nessa will." Arabella spoke as if she knew her words would never come true.

Cork leaned off the side of the bed and spat. "No shitein' chance there."

Arabella threw up her arms and swept out of the room. A moment later, she returned with Nessa in tow. The smaller woman's face was turned up in a sneer, but she'd come. Cork hadn't expected that. Perhaps she had a conscience somewhere under all that anger. Or Arabella had offered her money.

"And now yer both in my bedchamber, eh? Should I just bleedin' get dressed?"

Nessa scowled at Cork. "Milady Arabella has been crying all evening, making it quite difficult to sleep. When I suggested slitting her throat, she made it clear that talking to you might help her to shut her Kirthed mouth." She bared her teeth in an evil smile. "As much as I'd enjoy the silence, I'd prefer not to fight ten men at once. So I won't slit her throat yet. I need the job done first." Nessa's glare told Cork she wouldn't mind stabbing him in the eye as well.

Cork met Nessa's eyes and returned her glare. "I reckon I liked it better when you didn't talk."

"I reckon that like your ladylove—" Nessa gestured to Arabella— "you'd be easier to deal with if you had no tongue left."

"The people we're killin'," Cork said, ignoring Nessa's threats, "well, they're just tryin' to help some refugees." He inclined his head toward Arabella. "Arabella feels bad about killin' 'em, but I told her that's the job."

Arabella nodded. "We need to do something about this. Talk this through. It's not too late."

Nessa squinted at Arabella. "We have a job. We do the job."

"These are good people!"

"You've met them once. You hardly know that. And good people die all the time." Nessa's nose twitched. "My parents were good people. Didn't stop them from being slaughtered."

"Nessa, I—"

"I don't want your pity, girl. I want to do the godsdamned job."

"Nessa's right." Cork pushed himself up to sitting. "No point in arguin'." And no point in pressing Nessa for details either. The woman was already headed for the door.

"But the Winn are—" Arabella began.

"A buncha bastards." Cork stared daggers at her. "But those bastards have nothin' to do with this. Meldred said kill, so we kill."

"I just—"

"If ya need to cry, go cry. Ain't nothin' gonna change, girl." Cork's stomach clenched at the look of betrayal on Arabella's face, but it had to be done. Nessa didn't need to know about the Winn, and Arabella needed to shut up. "Now, get out of my room so I can get some kirthdamned sleep."

The next morning, Cork loaded up their hired horses and prepped for the journey into the Frozen Lands. Ruckels stood across the inn's courtyard, packing down his own horses, so it was impossible to avoid him completely, but Cork kept himself busy and refused to meet the man's eyes, even when Ruckels waved at him and called out a hello. What would Cork say? *Hello, I'm going to be killin' you later. Fancy sharing an ale?*

Ale did sound good, though. While Cork returned to the inn to purchase a few bottles for the journey, Ruckels, Myrna, and Torston set off to the west.

Cork, Arabella, and Nessa hurried to their own horses and followed, careful to stay far enough back to remain unseen. Every now and then, Nessa would spur her horse forward to scout the scene ahead and confirm they were still on Ruckels' trail. Arabella remained several yards behind Cork, sulking. She'd not said anything all morning, and Cork cursed himself for feeling a pang of sadness about pushing her away the night before.

When they'd traveled for around an hour, Arabella moved her horse up beside his. "We could fight the Winn." Arabella's voice took on a note of desperation.

Cork couldn't help smiling. "The Winn would slaughter us."

"You're good with your axe, Nessa's lethal with her daggers, and I—"

"Have you ever seen the Winn fight?"

Arabella shook her head. "No, but—"

"What about a mage?"

"Yes." Arabella swallowed. "I saw a mage send ice shards through a man's throat. Killed him instantly."

"The Winn are ten times as powerful as that. I dunno what it is—my mum always said somethin' in the water—but their powers are heightened. One Winn mage can defeat three regular mages. And the wolvinn, they'll rip a man's throat out with ease."

"But, you went right up to one!"

"Aye, but I wasn't tryin' to kill her masters."

"I'm just trying to fix the situation."

"No fixin' left."

"You're insufferable." Arabella spurred her horse forward, kicking dust up in her wake.

The Frozen Lands lived up to their name. Jagged cliffs of stark black rock looming above an all-encompassing gray. The ground was covered in ice, snow, and a mixture of the two, with only a few hearty brownish shrubs growing in patches. Perched on the cliffside, Cork watched for movement. Wind pelted his face, and even clad in a heavy fur-lined coat, he couldn't stop shivering.

"Why would anyone travel through this place?" Arabella asked from beside him.

Cork shrugged. Kirth knew why anyone would voluntarily come here. To this land where hope died. Where a man's balls were likely to turn to stone and fall off in the night. No one would last more than a few days out here.

"Over there." Nessa gestured toward the forest, away from the road, where two wolvinn drank from a pond. "They're massive."

"Yep," Cork said. *Turnos' tits.* He'd known the Winn would be watching but hoped they'd do a better job of staying out of sight. "Wolvinn, innit. Belong to the Winn."

"What in Kirth are the Winn doing this far from the Isle? Did they need new babies to eat?"

Arabella opened her mouth to respond.

"Dunno," Cork grunted. "I expect they're tryin' to get outta the damned cold, eh? Travel wherever it is they're goin'."

"You're Winn, though."

"Not anymore." *Not ever, really.*

Nessa furrowed her brow and eyed Cork's Dreamshapes.

"Aye, I've got the markings. Don't make me a Winn, though." He gave a wicked smile. "Ain't eaten a baby in months, have I?"

Nessa shuddered and looked away. "My parents were killed by mages. They were traders out along the Trunellic border with Rosenfel. One of the mages took a shine to my mother, and when my father objected, they slit his throat with their ice shards. My mother wouldn't stop screaming, so they killed her as well. I sat in the carriage, watching." Nessa clenched her jaw. "I was seven."

Bugger. The last thing Cork had expected was to feel sympathetic toward Nessa. "I can't imagine watchin' that."

Nessa's eyes moved to Cork's Dreamshapes. "I'd be fine if all mages died."

And just like that, Cork's sympathy dissipated. He clenched his teeth. "Well, my mum's a mage, and she's bleedin' dyin' right now. Never killed nobody." Cork squeezed his hands into fists. "I'm sorry mages killed yer parents, but you ain't got no right to blame them all."

"If only I cared what you thought." Nessa stood and moved several paces down the cliff, turning her back to Cork.

"What was that about?" Arabella asked, moving closer to sit beside Cork.

"She's just a shitein' delight, that's all."

"You really ought not to antagonize her like that."

"I didn't say nothin'. She just hates mages."

"Does she dislike mages more than everyone else?"

"Killed her parents. She was seven."

Arabella inhaled sharply. "That's beastly. I...well, I can't imagine going through something like that." She looked to Nessa, who had crouched to the ground and begun stabbing the ice with her daggers. "It almost makes sense why she's like that."

"Bleedin' insane."

"Emotionally wounded."

"Same thing."

After almost an hour of waiting, the convoy made its way onto the stretch of road below the cliffs. Six horse-drawn carts covered in linen tarps and at least five armed guards on horseback, Ruckels and Myrna among them, though Torsten was no where to be seen.

Good, stay far away, Torsten. Then I won't have to kill ya. The convoy was still a decent distance away, but Cork's shoulders tensed. Soon, he'd be slaughtering innocents. If his mother knew, would she have begged him not to go through with it? *I reckon I'm a murderer after all.*

Cork stood, brushing away any last lingering bits of shame. It was time to kill.

"Wait." Arabella grasped Cork's forearm. "There's a lot more of them than us."

"I'm good with my axe."

"I have an idea."

"I told you, we don't need no plans. We go in and kill—"

"Would you shut your bloody mouth and stop being such a man? You're not the only one with a say, Cork. I realize Meldred put you in charge, but you're being a complete prick right now, and I, for one, am tired of it!"

Cork stared at Arabella, mouth slightly ajar. Her eyes were steel, her jaw clenched. Kirth, she was beautiful. *This is why you shouldn't have told her about your mum, Cork. Looked into those hazel eyes of hers. Now yer feelin' things.* Cork sighed. "Shitein' bollocks, Arabella, I'm sorry."

"You've got about a minute before I start stabbing," Nessa said.

Cork motioned to Arabella. "Better talk fast."

"I'm a lady," Arabella began.

"I know that," Cork grunted. *Gods, do I know that.*

"What I mean is that, if our targets came upon a damsel in the Frozen Lands, alone and in distress, well, they might lower their guard and rush to assist said lady." Arabella grinned, pointing to Cork's axe. "And then, while they're distracted, the two of you can do what you do best."

Nessa furrowed her brow. "But Ruckels has seen you."

"He thinks I'm a woman traveling west for love. If I, with tears in my eyes, inform them that my dear betrothed has been murdered, and I only just escaped, well, Ruckels is a decent man. He'll help us."

"Ya think ya can pull this off?" Cork grimaced, thinking of Arabella's inability to deal with the three thugs back in Kilnic. "You don't got the best history with dealin' with people."

"Oh, Connick, you need not worry. I'll whimper and sniff my way into their hearts, and then you can send your blades into their skulls."

Nessa shrugged. "I hate to say it, but milady Arabella has a decent idea."

Arabella gave a mock bow. "Thanks ever so much."

"I still want to knife you."

"Fine," Cork said. "We'll do it your way, Arabella."

Arabella stood on her tiptoes and brushed her lips across Cork's own. "Let's do our best not to die, Connick."

While Cork watched from the forest, Arabella approached the convoy, dress torn and hair disheveled, her curls falling over the red of her cheek.

The horseman at the front, a weasel-faced man, called for the convoy to halt and peered down at Arabella. "State your business," he called down in an imperious voice.

"Oh, thank the Swordsman," Arabella cried. "I thought I would surely perish. I've been wandering the Frozen Lands for hours now and haven't seen a soul."

"Who are you?" The man sneered. "I didn't know there was a brothel in the Frozen Lands."

"I—" Arabella pulled at her dress to cover her exposed neckline from the man's leering gaze. "Bandits attacked us. They—" Arabella burst into tears.

"What's the holdup?" Myrna rode forward, hand on the hilt of her sword as if she expected trouble. When she saw Arabella, she pulled her horse to a halt and dismounted. "Arabella, is that you?" She stepped forward. The weasel-faced man dismounted and stood beside her.

Surprising. Myrna remembered Arabella's name. Apparently, the woman had an eye for detail.

"Myra, was it?" Arabella fell to her knees. "Gods, I'm tired." She fluttered, as if on the verge of fainting.

"What happened to you?" Myrna asked. She knelt, placing her hands on Arabella's shoulders to steady her. The weasel-faced man also knelt and put his hand on Arabella's, stroking it gently. Cork felt an irrational urge to rush out of the forest and axe the man then and there. He reached for the axe but stopped. *No, calm down, ya fool. Let her work.*

Arabella rubbed at her eyes and sighed theatrically. "My betrothed is dead. They slit his throat. Kirth knows what they would have done if I had not fled." She raised her eyes at them imploringly. "Will you help me?"

The man leered at her and puffed his chest out. "Aye, ma'am. I'll be glad to help you. Course, I'd help you even more if you make it worth my while afterward."

"Curtin," Myrna snarled. She smacked him across the back of the head. "She's just watched her betrothed die."

"Why in Kirth have we stopped?" Ruckels peered out from within the first cart of the convoy.

"You remember Arabella?" Myrna asked. "She needs help."

"Swordsman's tears." Ruckels climbed out of the cart and moved to Arabella's side. "Are you injured?"

"No," Arabella said, her voice fluttering as she shuddered. "But I am feeling quite faint." She collapsed into Ruckels' arms.

"Not a bad actress, that one." Nessa's voice came from behind Cork's ear, and he fought the urge to jump or call out. "Too bad she might die today. That would ruin your little love affair."

"Bugger off."

Ruckels carried Arabella to the cart and placed her on the driver's bench. He and Myrna crowded around her, administering to her.

There was no going back now. Only thing left to do was finish the job. Cork unsheathed his axe. All the convoy guards were facing away from him. He stepped out into the clearing, Nessa sliding by him and slinking along the forest edge.

Cork was almost to the first man when the convoy guards noticed him.

"What—" Cork's axe severed the man's neck, ending the cry.

A man gurgled and fell on the other side of the convoy, and suddenly the carts were in flames. Nessa stepped back from the burning cart, shooting Cork a wicked smile. Where in Kirth had she gotten the fire?

Ruckels and Myrna turned to Cork, mouths agape, blinking wildly. "Cork?" Ruckels grabbed at the hilt of his sword. "I thought you were dead."

"Yeah." Cork advanced. "Sorry 'bout that." He looked to Arabella. "Go!"

Myrna reached for the other woman, but Arabella disappeared under the linen cover and into the cart. Myrna climbed after her. Hopefully, there would be an exit on the other side. Otherwise, Arabella would be at Myrna's mercy.

"I thought you were a friend." Ruckels stepped forward, longsword in hand. He held the sword with practiced grace.

No doubt he was quite the swordsman, but Cork hadn't ever met anyone he couldn't defeat with his axe. "I called you our savior."

Ruckels bent a knee and sent forth a half thrust. Nothing Cork could handle.

"I's didn't ask ya to."

"I said you were a damned hero." Ruckels swung a heavy cut with the longsword, but Cork parried it easily with the haft of his axe. Cork stepped forward, leaning his weight onto his left foot, and brought the axe down in a cut of his own. Ruckels kept the blade from piercing his skull but stumbled. Cork could have ended him right then. Brought the axe down and cleaved Ruckels' in two. And yet, he paused for just too long, thinking of Arabella and what she'd said. How Ruckels seemed a good man.

Turnos' tits. Cork tried to push the emotions away.

"You're just a killer," Ruckels spat, leaning onto his back foot and half thrusting his sword at Cork.

Cork swatted the sword away. "I said I was just a man."

"Why are you doing this?"

"It's my job. Destroy the supplies. Kill the witnesses."

"I hope you suffer under Kirth's judgment, Cork, if that's even your name."

I'm sure I will. "I have to let one man survive. That can be you, Ruckels."

Another thrust, another parry. "I'd rather die. However, I hope you die first."

"I don't want to do this."

"You've lied enough already, you cur!" Ruckels heaved his blade in an off-balance thrust. Cork sidestepped the blow, moved his hand higher on the haft of his axe, and brought it down into Ruckels' shoulder. Blood sprayed into Cork's face as Ruckels collapsed, taking a few final gasps before his inevitable end.

Cork sighed and stepped over the body, willing the bile rising in his throat to stay down. There were more innocents to kill today. Cork's boots were stained red, and there was no way to know whose blood it was. Nothing to do but keep killing. He moved toward the convoy, where Nessa faced off against an armored man with a sad excuse for an axe, shorter than Cork's by half and showing signs of rust.

"No!" A strangled cry came from behind Cork. Cork turned to see Torsten running toward him, carrying only a dagger. Cork gripped the axe tight enough to turn his fingers white. Torsten was only a boy, for Kirth's sake. "Godsdamn you!" Torsten screamed, eyes wide, flicking wildly between his father's body and Cork.

Aye, the gods do damn me. "I—" Cork broke off as Torsten lunged at him with the dagger. *I won't kill you, boy,* Cork had been about to say, but he knew it was a lie. He'd kill Torsten if he had to. Anything for his mother.

"You bastard! You fucking bastard!"

Cork only nodded. He lifted the axe. "I was tellin' yer da that I have to let one man live. It can be you, boy."

Torsten lunged again, the dagger missing Cork by several inches.

"I'm going to kill you," the boy said through gritted teeth. "I won't stop until you're dead." He readied another attack.

Cork took a step back. "Run. Live to hate me another day."

Torsten raised the dagger and let out a wild howl of despair.

Cork brought his axe down into Torsten's head, the blade cleaving the boy's skull with a sickening crunch.

Cork's stomach clenched. Thankfully, he'd not eaten yet that day, or he would have been sick. *No time for remorse. Gotta finish the job.*

Across the clearing, the axe-wielding man lay bleeding out. Nessa had moved on to Myrna. An evenly matched bout, Myrna's longsword against Nessa's blades. But Nessa moved faster. Within moments, Myrna lay on the ground, gurgling as blood escaped her slit throat. Nessa scurried after the weasel-faced man, Curtin. Cork shuddered at Nessa's grim smile.

In the midst of the battle, Cork had lost track of Arabella. She was nowhere to be seen. Had she been injured or killed? Myrna could have caught her and slain her before moving on to die at Nessa's hand.

A rustle of movement behind him broke Cork out of his thoughts. He turned his head to see a dagger moving toward his face. A woman, barely taller than Nessa. There wasn't enough time to move. The dagger would hit, but if Cork leaned back, perhaps the dagger would only ravage his cheek instead of entering his skull.

Cork waited for the pain, but it didn't come. An arrow whistled through the air and lodged in the woman's throat, the dagger falling harmlessly over Cork's shoulder as the woman fell.

Following the arrow's path, Cork saw Arabella, face scrunched up, preparing another arrow for flight. She gave Cork a half-grimacing wink, then returned to her task, scanning the clearing for more targets.

The ice ran red as Cork stalked across the clearing toward the last few men. Nessa had taken down at least three of the convoy guards, and now she had Curtin backed up against a tree.

"I'm sorry," Curtin wailed. He reached his arms out in a feeble attempt to block Nessa's daggers.

However, Nessa knelt to one knee and brought her daggers up through Curtin's face, just below his chin. He gasped, opening his mouth to scream but only dribbling blood down his lips and into Nessa's hair.

Nessa hopped to her feet and turned to Cork. "Who's left?"

Cork indicated the fiery wreckage of the convoy. "Two of 'em went running back that way."

Nessa said nothing, sprinting behind the burning carts and out of sight. Cork lifted his axe and rolled his eyes.

Axes weren't the best weapon for running. He took off after Nessa.

What he saw on the other side of the convoy made his heart thump in his chest. He stopped running and stared on, mouth open, trying to breathe. Three figures sat huddled together, shivering as Nessa approached.

A woman and two children, neither of whom could be older than twelve.

"Nessa," Cork hissed. Nessa advanced, daggers flashing in the two suns. "Nessa, wait, godsdammit."

"We have a job," Nessa muttered. "We do it."

"They're bleedin' children."

"So was I." Nessa's fingers gripped her daggers even tighter. "And I wish I had died then." She gave a ragged sigh. "It would have made things so much easier."

There was no reason to try to talk Nessa out of it. If Cork stood still, the children would be dead within the next few moments.

"Shitein' bollocks." Cork lowered his axe to his side and ran.

Nessa must have heard his lumbering footsteps because she stopped and faced him, daggers at the ready. Her jaw was clenched, her face expressionless. "I'll kill you if I have to, Cork."

Cork lifted his axe but stopped out of Nessa's reach.

The woman stood up in front of the two children. "I won't let you hurt them. You're monsters, all of you."

Cork nodded. "Aye."

The woman took a small, rusted knife from the folds of her skirts. She inhaled deeply and lunged for Nessa.

The woman never had a chance. Without even looking back, Nessa buried a dagger into the woman's neck, blood spurting out onto Nessa's face. The woman fell, whimpering as she slowly died.

"Ma!" the older of the two children yelled. As one, the children lunged for their fallen mother.

"Only one more left to kill." Nessa's eyes never left Cork. "If you'd like, you can decide which of them lives."

"We're not killin' kids," Cork said.

Nessa smirked. "You've already killed one boy today, Cork."

The bile rose once again. "Ya, well, I'm done."

"Wait!" Arabella yelled from behind Cork. "I have an idea."

"Go to Kirth, your ladyship."

In response, Arabella took an arrow from her quiver and lined it up in her bow, pointing straight at Nessa's face.

"You can try to shoot me," Nessa said, still smirking. "But if you miss, your lover here will get a dagger in the eye."

"I'm not..." Cork started. Her lover? Going to die?

"You might be decent with that axe, Cork, but I'm faster. And speed outweighs strength."

"Go ahead and try."

"Gods, would you both shut up?" Arabella said with an exasperated sigh. "We can still walk away from this, all alive. These children and us." She swallowed. "We pretend to kill one of them. Tell them to stay down for a bit. After a while, once the Winn have gone, they can escape."

"What do the Winn have to do with this?"

"They hired us," Cork said. "We've been workin' fer 'em all along. Mages."

Arabella lowered her bow. "We can still stop this, Nessa."

"Get buggered," Nessa said. With a speed Cork hadn't realized she possessed, Nessa slid past him before he could even bring his axe back into position to swing. She wasn't going for the children, though. She charged at Arabella, only pausing to evade the arrow Arabella sent her way.

Cork watched on, mute and horrified, as Nessa brought a dagger down into Arabella's chest, just to the left of her shoulder. He was only a few paces away, but his legs refused to move.

Arabella opened her mouth in a shocked gasp and tumbled to the icy ground.

There was no time to check if she was still breathing. No time to do anything but finish this. As Cork pushed the shock from his mind, Nessa knelt beside Arabella and moved to slit her throat.

Cork roared, charging Nessa with his axe at the ready. Nessa sprang to her feet and stepped away from the bleeding Arabella. There was blood everywhere, but Cork saw Arabella's body trembling as she breathed in weakly. Alive for now.

Cork slowed his charge. "I didn't want to kill you."

"Funny. I *really* want to kill you."

Nessa stepped to the side, then dropped into a crouch, somersaulting Cork's blade as he heaved his axe toward her. She rose to one knee and brought her dagger down into Cork's thigh at the crease in his armor, a weak spot. Pain seared through him, but he pushed it away. It would have to wait.

She made to stand and no doubt drive her other dagger into Cork's skull, but he moved faster.

A knee to Nessa's head.

A kick to her stomach.

A boot on her throat.

Cork swayed. He knew what he had to do. He'd never killed a coworker before. Always soldiers or nameless thugs. But today was a day of firsts.

At least she wasn't innocent.

Nessa gurgled from below. She drove a dagger into his leg, just above the ankle. Cork pressed his boot down harder. He wanted to break her godsdamned neck. Stomp her head until her skull lay shattered.

The way he felt.

But he was a professional.

And he had an axe for a reason.

"Go to Kirth." Cork brought the axe down into Nessa's skull, severing it just above the hairline. Blood splashed his boots, but he didn't care. He lifted the axe and brought it down again. A third time. He raised it again.

"Cork," Arabella whispered.

Shit. Cork dropped the axe and moved to her. "Ara. Yer stayin' alive, ya hear?"

Arabella's lips curled, not into a smile, but into the closest possible thing when wounded like she was.

"The job." Arabella's eyes moved past his.

Cork looked back at the two children, who knelt over the dead woman. Cork picked up one of Nessa's daggers. "Look," he said to the children. "I'm gonna pretend to kill one of ya. Lie there like yer dead for a while, then get the hell outta here."

"What?" The older boy crossed his arms. "Why would we trust a murderer?"

"Ya want to live? Just pretend to be dead." Cork stepped forward and grabbed the younger boy. "This won't hurt."

The older boy screamed and charged at Cork. Cork slung an arm out and threw the boy to the ground. He knelt beside the older boy and brought forth the dagger, gently swiping it across the boy's neck, inches above his skin. "Lie there fer a bit, now," Cork said quietly. "Once I'm gone, wait a while longer. Then take one of the remaining horses and ride fer the nearest town. There's one not more than an hour west of here."

The boy spat in Cork's face. "Kirth take you."

"He will. Gods, he will."

Cork stood and moved to Arabella, scooping her up in his arms. She moaned as he placed her on his shoulder. After dropping the dagger on Nessa's corpse, Cork carried Arabella to their horses, placing her on the horse's back and then mounting the beast. He lifted Arabella into his lap, cradling her.

Stay alive.

Cork spurred the horse forward. If the gods still watched over him, and they weren't too angry with his sins this day, perhaps he'd find a medic in time.

PART FOUR:

FACING THE CONSEQUENCES

THE ROOM AT THE inn felt smaller now, even with the medic hovering over Arabella, who lay unconscious on the bed, breathing shallowly. Cork sat on a rickety wooden chair in the corner, staring out the window, trying to ease the swirling emotions in his head and the churning pit in his stomach. He'd failed the mission. If the Winn found out, they'd kill his mother. Arabella might die as well.

All he'd needed to do was kill one of the children. Then he and Arabella would be safe, and Nessa would still be alive. His mother would be saved.

One quick cut with his axe. He'd already killed one boy; what was another death? But he couldn't do it. He couldn't bloody do it.

And now everything had gone to shit.

"Your wife will live. I think." The medic's voice shook Cork from his downward spiral. "She may never regain the usage of her arm, though."

Cork nodded. "Thank ya." The tumult in his stomach eased slightly.

"The faster you get her to Kilnic, the more she may recover. There's only so much I can do here with what little supplies I have."

Cork reached down to grasp Arabella's pale hand. Kirth, it was colder than the Frozen Lands.

"She'll be too weak to move on her own for several days," the medic continued. "Good luck, sir."

Arabella whimpered and then began to wheeze. Cork brushed strands of hair from her gaunt face, lingering on her cheek.

Swordsman, let her live. Kirth, Torr, if any of you are listening, let her live.

After paying the medic, Cork loaded Arabella and their supplies on the horse. No carriages this time around. A horse would get to Kilnic almost a day faster.

They passed by the inn in Turnosis where a goose had tried to bite Arabella only a few days before. It felt like ages ago now. Cork didn't stop. There would be no rest until he'd made it home.

The crunch of gravel under hooves brought an unbidden image to Cork's mind. Torsten, looking up at him, eyes wide, as the axe split his head open. Blade grinding against skull, blood and brain matter leaking from the wound. Cork shuddered and spurred the horse on.

After a day and a half of travel, only stopping to water or switch horses in the settlements along the way, they arrived back in Kilnic. Cork maneuvered the horse through the crowds of the markets and rode past the Cross without a second glance. Meldred would be upset that Cork didn't report to him as soon as he returned, but Meldred could choke on his bollocks.

When they reached Cork's mother's house, Cork dismounted, took Arabella in his arms, and carried her up the steps.

Arabella opened her eyes, giving Cork the ghost of a smile. "Hello," she murmured.

Cork rapped at the door with his boot, and after a long moment, his mother opened the door. She looked skinnier than when he'd left, but her sores had healed somewhat, no doubt because of the tonic Cork had purchased before he'd left for the Frozen Lands.

"Mum," Cork would have pulled his mother into a hug; however, he still had Arabella in his arms.

"Hello, Mrs. Connick." Arabella's voice, though shaky, still had her trademark sauciness.

Cork's mother looked to Cork. "Who's this?"

"Arabella. She's..." Cork looked down at Arabella's pale face. "Well, she's important to me, and I need to get her a medic."

"Lay her down here." His mother pointed to a padded chair. "I'll watch her. You get the medic."

Cork did so. After a quick hug for his mother, he rushed back out into the streets.

Before he could walk more than a few steps, Trellen and Yannel Winn blocked his path, black robes flowing in the brisk afternoon air. *Bastard bleedin' shite.*

"Corkelle Winn?" Yannel's face stayed a calm mask.

Cork eyed the woman. "It's just Cork."

A slight bow. "As you wish, Corkelle Winn."

"What d'ya want?"

"You failed in what you were hired to do."

"I killed 'em all."

Trellen shook his head, almost sadly. "Two children lived. We watched your deception, Corkelle Winn. You insult the Flock with your failure."

"I don't count it as failure."

"Your penance increases." Yannel's eyes lowered.

"Kirth take my penance. I'm never going back to the damned Isle."

"Your mother grows ill."

"Just sell me the godsdamned tonic."

Trellen frowned. "Your betrayal of the Flock must be punished. However, we understand your weakness. Children are a gift from the Swordsman."

"Uh, thank ya, I s'pose. Ya dirty bastards."

Trellen remained stone-faced. "We shall not impede your mother's health. We shall not give you tonic, but you may continue to purchase it from the medics about town."

Yannel furrowed her brow. "However, do not lie to us again, or we will not be so kind. In that case, your mother will die, Corkelle Winn. And it will be your fault."

"Bug—" Cork stopped himself. *Bugger off*, he'd been about to say. But this situation called for diplomacy. "I, uh, I thank the Winn—I mean the Flock. Yer a buncha gods-damned saviors."

Kirth. Saviors. Images of Ruckels flashed through Cork's mind. Laughter, kindness, the inevitable disappointment, and the even more inevitable death.

"You must leave Kilnic." Yannel eyed Cork dispassionate-ly. "To stay spells doom upon your mother."

"What?"

"We shall not kill your mother, but you must serve your penance. You will depart at once."

"I'm not leavin' my bleedin' mum!"

"Then you both shall perish."

Cork started to reach for his axe. It would be so easy to swing at the Winn, get an ice shard through the throat or eye, and bleed out on the street. To die in one last attempt to save his mother, no matter how doomed the attempt.

As his hand brushed against the pommel, he paused. His mother would die, and he would die. But what of Arabella? He'd promised to get a medic for her, and if he died on the street now, Kirth knew how long it would be before someone checked on his mother. Arabella was too weak to move. She'd starve to death or die from lack of treatment or infection.

Another idea flashed into Cork's mind. He lowered his hands and eyed the Winn, both of whom held their own hands up, ready to end his life with the damned magic.

"Alright," Cork said. "You win. I'll leave." He turned to walk away but paused. "You lot are a buncha pricks."

Cork didn't look back. He half expected the Winn to murder him on the street, but no, that wasn't their style. They just hired desperate people to murder for them.

Bugger them all. And bugger me too.

After retrieving the medic, Cork led the man back to his mother's rooms. Meldred stood waiting for him outside the door, scowling and tossing a coin anxiously.

"What in Kirth's name, Cork?" Meldred caught the coin and squeezed.

"Go on in." Cork motioned to the medic to enter the rooms, then turned to Meldred and gave a tired grin. "I did the job, innit?"

"Hardly. The Winn are angry."

"To Kirth with the Winn." *And with ye.*

"Where are Nessa and Arabella?"

"Arabella's in there." Cork nodded toward the rooms. "Wounded."

"Pity," Meldred shrugged. "Ah, well. That's mercenary life for you. And Nessa?"

"Dead."

Meldred pursed his lips. "Interesting. I thought she was better than that. To be killed by a mere convoy guard."

"I killed her."

Meldred chuckled mirthlessly. "Good riddance, there. But damn it, Cork, you've ruined the company."

Cork stood tall, peering down at Meldred. "I's don't give a shit, boss. I'm leavin' town."

"What? First you cause the Winn to blacklist my services, and now you're leaving? You're my best employee, gods-dammit."

"I reckon I quit."

Meldred blinked rapidly. "I made you who you are, you miserable whelp." He opened and closed his mouth, then sneered. "Your whore mother deserves to die."

Cork unsheathed his axe. "I'll not kill ya. Just this once."

"Get out of Kilnic, then. If you ever come back, I'll make sure you join your mother in death."

Gods, he wanted to slice Meldred's mouth from his face. But killing the man wouldn't solve anything. Not when there had already been so much death. He bent his elbow and brought the handle of the axe into Meldred's nose, grinning at the sound of a crack and the rush of blood.

Meldred moaned, and Cork brought the handle down against Meldred's skull. Meldred slumped to the ground, unconscious but still breathing. Cork gave him a kick to the stomach, then stepped over his former employer and entered the rooms.

The medic stood over Arabella, pouring a thick purple liquid onto her wounds and massaging it in. A pain reliever, made from mage-infused water, which the medic had used on Cork many times after he'd picked up a wound on the job. It didn't heal anything but eased the pain long enough for the medic to do the real work: reaching into the wound with his mage powers, pulling the infected blood out, and then suturing it closed.

Cork shuddered. The way mages could manipulate blood just like water had always terrified him, even when it was his mother cleaning up one of his bloody noses. *It was unnatural,* he'd thought then, before cursing himself for calling his own mother unnatural.

There was little Cork could do for Arabella besides wait. He joined his mother by the hearth and took a swig from a jug of ale his father had no doubt left out that morning.

"I'm mighty tired," his mother said. "Mind takin' me to my bed?"

Cork lifted her and carried her into her bedroom, gently placing her down on the bed. "Anything I can get for ya, Mum?"

"Well, boy, tell me about the girl." She gave a wan smile.

"Her name's Arabella."

"You told me that earlier. Are the two of you lovers?"

Cork choked on his own spittle. "Swordsman's bloody tears, Mum!"

"She's a pretty thing, that lass. You'd best do whatever ya need to get her, well, in the family way."

"Mum, I—" Cork inhaled, trying to think of what to say. "Mum, you's can't talk like that." He glanced toward Arabella, but the medic blocked his view. "She's a lady."

"What, I'm trying to make sure I'm gonna have grandchildren, aren't I, boy?" Her eyes lowered to her lap, where her pale hands trembled. "I'm not going to live much longer, you know."

"Mum, yer gonna live for years." Cork tried to look her in the eyes but couldn't. Lying to his mother had always been bleedin' difficult. "We're leavin' Kilnic. Go somewhere else, where no one knows us. I'll keep workin', and we'll buy the tonic. Yer gonna live."

His mother's jaw clenched. "I ain't leaving Kilnic."

"Mum, you'll die here without me takin' care of ya. Yer comin' with me, no arguments."

"Better to die here than in some far-off, foreign land. This is my home, and I'll stay here. If you force me to travel with you against my will, I vow I will no longer take the tonic. I will waste away."

"Mum, ya don't understand, the Winn—"

"The Winn don't scare me, boy. I'm Winn, too."

"I'm stayin' too, then."

She reached out to take his hand. "If you stay, I will also refuse the tonic. Corkelle, go into the world, make a difference."

Cork blew out a breath. His mother had left him little choice in the matter. "I'll send money back, Mum."

Cork leaned down and hugged her. She sobbed gently against his shoulder, and Cork blinked away tears of his own. After a few minutes, his mother's breathing turned slower and finally into snores. Cork laid her down in the chair and kissed her forehead.

"And I will save ya somehow."

When Cork walked back out into the sitting room, Arabella lay sprawled in a chair, watching him, the slightest bit of color returned to her cheeks.

"How is she?" Arabella asked.

"'Bout as you'd expect." Cork sat down in the chair the medic had vacated next to Arabella.

"So, she'll live?"

"As long as she gets the tonic still." Cork sighed. "That's the shitein' problem."

"The Winn?"

"Aye. And Meldred. They're not happy."

"I wouldn't assume they would be. What are you planning?"

"I's have to leave the city. Maybe the country."

"Oh." Arabella inhaled deeply. "You're leaving."

"I's got to. Bloody Winn will make my life hell otherwise."

"I see." Arabella played with the hem of her dress.

"Do ya..." Cork lowered his eyes. "Do ya want to travel with me?"

"As opposed to what?" Arabella's eyes glinted, and the corners of her lips tipped up.

"I reckon ya could stay here. Meldred blames me fer what happened in the Frozen Lands. I'd understand if ya want to. Stay here, that is. Yer family's here after all—"

"Connick, stop talking." Arabella took Cork's hand in hers. "I told you from the beginning that I didn't want to be a cobbler. I wanted to travel. To make—" she faltered. "To make a living with my bow. Well, that's not happening any longer. The medic told me I'll never shoot a bow again."

"Ya don't know that."

"I have to be realistic. Cork, I need you to listen to me. I'll be a hindrance to you. I won't be able to fight off anyone. I'll never be a mercenary."

"I know that."

"And I can't do that to you. You don't deserve that. Not with your mother sick like she is. I assume she's coming with you where you go?"

"No," Cork bit out. "She's stayin' here, no matter what." He squeezed Arabella's hand. Too hard. She winced. "Sorry." He moved his hand to his side. "She won't leave, but I've got to. Look for work, send the money here to her. It's the only way."

Arabella reached out to take Cork's hand in hers. "That's just another reason why I shouldn't go with you. You need to send the money to her, not waste it supporting me." She smiled sadly. "Where are you going, anyway?"

"Rosenfel to begin with. There's bound to be work there. And if I need to, I'll head west to Oban. They're always fightin' someone. I'm sure they pay soldiers well."

"Gods, I can't imagine living in Oban."

"I want ya to come with me, Arabella." Cork's voice broke when he spoke her name. For the second time that day, liquid welled in his eyes.

Arabella bit the inside of her cheek, then smiled. The cold pit in Cork's stomach warmed.

"I suppose I'll travel with you," Arabella said. "Some of the way, at least. I've always wanted to go to Dramin. See the sights, the fashion, the culture. I won't ever be a mercenary, but I could carve a life out there. So, if you're traveling that way, I'll go with you." She pulled Cork down into a kiss, then moved her lips to his ear. "And Connick, thank you for saving me. I still think you're infuriating."

She kissed him again. And for a moment, that's all that mattered.

Then Arabella shrieked. Cork jumped to his feet. "What?"

"My arm. You were crushing it."

"I'm sorry." Cork looked toward his mother's room. Hopefully she hadn't been awoken by the screams. "I 'spose we should get packed."

"Connick, come here." Arabella winked at him. "But this time, steer clear of my arm."

The next morning, Cork and Arabella set off with a horse and cart; Cork drove the cart while Arabella lay propped up on pillows in the back. She was far too weak to ride a horse at this point and spent much of the first day sleeping.

After a week of inns, rocky paths, and altogether too much snow, they reached Rosenfel, where the trees began to grow taller.

"It's beautiful," Arabella said. Cork jumped. He'd thought she was asleep.

"Aye." Cork peered out into the virgin forest of tall pines interspersed here and there with yorn.

"It's quite freeing, you know. Being in Rosenfel."

Cork noticed movement in the forest. Something gray rushed behind the trees. An animal? He focused his eyes on the forest.

And there they were. The godsdamn Winn. At least four of them, and several wolvinn as well.

Watching.

"Don't you think it's freeing, Connick?"

I'll never be free. "Aye, bleedin' freein', ain't it?"

"What's wrong?"

"Nothin'." Cork looked away from the trees. There was nothing he could do. The Winn would follow him if they wished to. "Come on, let's get to kirthdamned Dramin."

Cork loosened the reins and urged the horses forward. He forced his mind away from the Winn and focused on the rhythmic thumping of hooves and wheels as the cart moved along the road.

Who knew what to expect? Arabella would go to Dramin and stay, and he would most likely move on, searching until he found work. They wouldn't be together much longer. Fleeting, like everything else in life.

Cork looked back at Arabella. Her eyes were closed again. Gods, she looked so beautiful. And most importantly, she was beautiful on the inside. Even if she was still bleedin' infuriating sometimes.

Frigid air assaulted Cork's face, but he didn't reach for a scarf or hat. The scent of pines made his senses tingle, and a light mist tickled his cheeks. Like Arabella said, it was freeing. Nothing was certain. Swordsman knew what the future held. But for now, it was enough.

ACKNOWLEDGEMENTS

Being an indie author is fun, but it's also incredibly stressful! Thankfully, I've had a lot of great people on my side!

So here's to you.

Special thanks to Caitlin, my wonderful wife. I love you, and I'm so grateful to you for putting up with me!

Audrie, who is always the first person I go to with my writing.

Rach, Sean, S.R., Greg, and Pete: thanks for your alpha/beta help!

Sam Parrish for her editing expertise.

My fellow Secret Scribes and Willow Wraith Press buddies. You make writing fun!

My parents, my brothers, and my friends. Also, all of my amazing drama students.

And of course, all the dogs in my life, especially my best girl, Rowena.

ABOUT THE AUTHOR

Dave Lawson is an Oklahoma-based fantasy novelist. He received an MFA in Fiction Writing from The New School in 2009 and published some contemporary literary fiction, before spending several years doing absolutely nothing with his degree. Now, he's returned to his first love--and what he enjoys reading--fantasy. His first fantasy novel, The Envoys of War, was released in October of 2024. He enjoys writing about conniving rakes and creative liars who do whatever they must to get what they desire. However, Dave's not like his characters. Pinky swear.

When he's not writing, he teaches high school English and Drama. He lives with his wife, Caitlin, and their dog, Rowena, who is a ball of energy. In a past life, Dave was surely a pirate.